Andy is the only one of his brothers who hasn't met his mate yet, and he doesn't expect it to happen anytime soon. What would be the odds? So he's stunned when he meets Claude and realizes he just did.

Claude had no idea what he was getting into when he agreed to go to a birthday party. He didn't expect his boss and father figure to tell him that he, his family, and his son-in-law's family are all shifters.

Claude has a hard time believing shifters are a thing outside romance novels, so Andy decides to wait to tell him about their bond. Then Claude asks him to be his fake boyfriend at a work event, and Andy can't say no. He hopes the experience will pull them together, but Claude has erected a hard shell around his heart, and he's not about to break it down.

Claude is done with relationships, so why does he want to give in to Andy? Why is he tempted to put his heart in jeopardy once again when he swore he'd never allow another man to make him vulnerable and hurt him?

Will Andy be the one to break down Claude's walls and convince him to trust his heart, or will he fail and find himself rejected by his mate?

This book is a work of fiction. Names, characters, places, and incidents either are products of the author's imagination or are used fictitiously. Any resemblance to actual events or locales or persons, living or dead, is entirely coincidental.

Trust the Heart
Copyright © 2022 Catherine Lievens
ISBN: 978-1-4874-3690-2
Cover art by Angela Waters

Published by eXtasy Books Inc

Look for us online at:
www.eXtasybooks.com

Trust the Heart
Seven Brothers 7

By

Catherine Lievens

CHAPTER ONE

Everything was changing.

Andy had known this would happen. One by one, his brothers had found their mates, and now they were happy and living their best life. Even Jack, who'd bitched and had tried to run away from Blair, had eventually given in.

And then, there was Andy.

He hadn't met his mate yet. He kept telling himself that he was young and had plenty of time, but when he saw his younger brother Laurie happy with his mate and their daughter, he couldn't help but wonder. Was he really too young to meet his mate? Laurie had turned twenty recently, but Andy was going on twenty-four, and he was still single. It had been easy to deal with when he and Jack were in the same situation, but they weren't anymore. The only brother who hadn't met his mate yet was Andy, and he wasn't sure how to deal with that.

He looked around the living room. It was Blair's birthday, and they were having a party at the home he and Jack shared. Blair had bought Jack his dream house, and while Jack had been pissed initially, he'd gotten over it. Jack needed his independence, even though he and Blair were together, and it was good to see he finally understood that having Blair buy him things didn't mean he wasn't independent. Blair had a lot of money and loved buying gifts, especially for his mate. It was one of the ways he showed Jack he cared.

"I know that look," a voice said.

Andy plastered a smile on his face and turned to his

1

mother. "What look?"

She squinted. "*That* look. You're trying hard to show everyone you're happy, but I know."

She had plenty of experience reading Andy's expressions. Sometimes he wished that wasn't true. Wasn't he allowed to pout in a corner for an hour or so? Everyone would understand, and beyond his mother, no one had bothered him. He should have known better than to think she'd allow it. She wanted Andy to be as happy as his brothers, but he wasn't sure it was in the cards for him, at least not at the moment.

"What's going on?" his mother asked.

Andy looked back at the spot where Jack and Blair were sitting. They were close together, with Jack's head leaning against Blair's shoulder. They were talking, and Jack suddenly laughed, loud and happy.

Andy couldn't remember seeing his brother that happy and at peace. No matter how much Jack resisted, it was good that he'd given in. Blair was his world, his mate, and they were so in love that it almost hurt to look at them.

But that was an Andy problem, not a Jack problem or something their mother should have to get involved in.

"Ah. I see." Andy's mother's voice was softer now. "Your time will come, too."

"I know." Although Andy wasn't too sure about that.

It was a miracle that all his brothers had met their mates. What would be the odds that he would, too? And even if, in the end, he did meet his mate, he doubted it would happen anytime soon. Jack and Blair had been together for a few months, but it would be too soon for Andy to meet his mate, right? With his luck, he'd meet the guy when he was eighty and couldn't walk without a cane. He supposed they could be happy for a few years, but he wanted more.

He wanted what his brothers had. He wanted someone to look at him the way Blair looked at Jack now. He wanted to celebrate birthdays and Christmases and Thanksgivings. He wanted an entire life with his mate, and he had no idea whether or not he'd get that.

"He's not going to abandon you just because he met his mate," Andy's mother said.

She'd been able to tell that Andy was moping over several things. Sometimes, how well she could read him and his brothers was scary, although he supposed it came with the territory. She had seven boys and had to learn how to read them before they did something they shouldn't.

"I know that, too," Andy told her.

And he really did. Jack had moved out of their shared apartment, and while it felt weird, it was natural. Jack was starting a new chapter of his life with Blair, a chapter where Andy didn't belong. That didn't mean they weren't brothers anymore or that they weren't close. Out of all of Andy's brothers, Jack was always the one he'd been the closest to. That wouldn't change just because Jack had found his mate.

But it wasn't easy to get used to all the changes. Andy felt like everything was moving too quickly, and he was scrambling to keep up. The problem was that Andy was the only one who *couldn't* keep up. All of his brothers were moving on with their lives, meeting their mates, and having children, but Andy was stuck. He lived in his old apartment, still had the same job, and hadn't met anyone. He wanted a relationship, but he was terrified that he'd meet his mate as soon as he found someone and things became serious with them. It would either be that or when he was eighty, and he wasn't sure he wanted to take that risk.

But on the other hand, could he stay single until he met his mate when he couldn't be a hundred percent sure that he'd eventually meet him? No matter how much he wished otherwise, there was no way for him to know. He might never meet his mate, and then what would he do? Was he supposed to be alone for the rest of his life?

His mother grabbed his hand and squeezed. "You're thinking too hard about this."

"How am I supposed to not think about it? Look around. You all have your mates, and you're all happy. Then there's me, the outsider."

His mother's expression turned fierce. "You are *not* an outsider. You're my son, and you're part of this family. I won't let you talk about yourself that way, and I don't care that you haven't met your mate. These are your people, and that's never going to change."

She was right. Whatever happened, Andy would never be alone because he'd always have his brothers. Things might be changing, but they weren't changing to the point that his brothers would stop caring about him.

Especially Jack. No matter what happened between Jack and Blair, Jack and Andy were still brothers and best friends. He'd made sure Andy knew that, but he hadn't needed to, because Andy did.

Besides, he wanted Jack to be happy. Blair made that happen, so what could Andy say about it? What could he say about any of this?

He smiled at his mother, and this time, it was more natural. "I know. I'm a bit down, but it'll pass."

His mother stared for a moment. "You can come to any of us if you need to talk. I realize that watching all of your brothers meet their mate while you're still on your own can't be easy, but who's to say you're not about to turn a corner and meet him? It could happen at any moment."

"Or it might never happen."

"Don't say that. You have to keep hoping. After all, who would've thought that both Laurie and Jack would meet their mate and be happy with them? Remember how against it Laurie was?"

Andy chuckled. Laurie had been telling anyone who listened that he didn't want a mate since he was thirteen or fourteen. Then he'd met Alexis, and he'd fallen in love.

"You'll be happy, too," Andy's mother continued. She pulled him closer and wrapped her arms around him. "You'll see. I have faith in your future and your mate." She pushed him away. "Now, why don't you help me in the kitchen?"

Andy laughed. "I thought Blair had forbidden you to help?"

"He's busy with your brother, and by the time he realizes what I'm doing, it'll be too late."

It wasn't like Andy had anything better to do, so he nodded and followed his mother to the kitchen. "Are we expecting more people?" he asked when he saw the massive amount of food spread out on the counters.

"Blair's parents are coming. I'm not sure about his sister, but he and Jack did a good thing, buying all this food. Knowing you and your brothers, there won't be a crumb left by the end of the evening."

She was probably right, and Andy got started by snatching a baby carrot and popping it into his mouth. His mother glared, but there was no heat behind it.

Whatever happened or didn't happen, Andy wasn't unhappy. How could he be when he had such a big family who loved him and filled his life with laughter and anything else he might want?

"I still don't understand why I had to come along," Claude grumbled from the back seat of Edgar's car.

Edgar and his wife, Mathilde, were in the front, with Edgar driving. They'd been silent, but Claude's gaze caught Edgar's in the rearview mirror.

"Why shouldn't you come home?" Edgar asked.

"Because I'm not family. I'm not part of any of this." Or at least, he shouldn't be.

Edgar snorted. "I see you more often than I see my children."

"That's because I work for you."

"Exactly. You're like a son to me, which means you're Blair's brother. It's his birthday, and he wanted us to be there."

"Lisa isn't here."

"Because she had something to do with her in-laws. Come on, Claude. Do you *have* to bitch all the way to Blair's house?"

Claude was tempted to say yes, but instead, he pressed his lips together.

Sometimes, it was hard to remember that Edgar was his boss. He'd given Claude a chance when he'd been looking for a personal assistant, even though Claude hadn't had any previous experience. Claude still didn't know how he'd gotten so lucky, but he had, and now he had a good job, a nice apartment, and he was living his best life.

The only sore spot was his mother, but Claude was used to dealing with her. She disliked the relationship he and Edgar had built, but Claude wasn't about to listen to her on that. Edgar was a surrogate father to him, and he couldn't give that up.

Dammit. He supposed he kind of *was* Blair's brother.

"Besides, don't you want to get to know Blair's new family?" Mathilde asked.

"I'm just not sure what they'll think of me being there."

"Blair and Jack invited you. That means they want you there."

Claude supposed that was right, but he still had no idea what he was doing here. It wasn't his place. No matter how close he was to Edgar, he wasn't part of the family. He already had his own family and had more than enough problems with his mother. He didn't need six surrogate brothers.

Because that was how many brothers Jack had. Jack and Blair were living together now, and Claude wouldn't be surprised if soon, they'd announce they were getting married. The thought of having so many brothers and so many people living in the same house blew his mind. It had always been him, his mother, and later, his sister. What was it like to grow up with six brothers? Claude couldn't even begin to wrap his mind around the mess and the noise, and he wondered how long he'd have to deal with it before he could escape the party.

Of course, even if he did manage to escape, he wouldn't be going anywhere, since he'd come with Edgar.

"There it is," Mathilde said.

Claude peered through the windshield to look at the house in front of them. It was cheery, even in the growing darkness. All the lights in the house seemed to be on, and Claude could see people through the window.

It was *a lot* of people.

Most of them were men. He supposed that made sense between the seven brothers and Blair.

Edgar parked in front of the house. He and Mathilde looked at each other, having the kind of silent conversation married people had. They'd been together a long time, and that love was still as strong as Claude imagined it had been when they'd first met. Mathilde nodded quickly, then climbed out of the car. As she did so, the front door opened, and Blair came out. He beamed at his mother and opened his arms, meeting her halfway down the porch steps. She hugged him, and Claude watched them, wondering why he'd never had that kind of relationship with his mother.

But the why didn't matter.

He opened his door and slid out of the car. The air was cold, which felt good after spending an hour in the car. He stretched, then moved toward the house to say hello to Blair.

Blair met him before he could reach him, and Claude watched as Mathilde quickly climbed the porch steps and disappeared into the house.

"Happy birthday," he told Blair.

Blair's smile was gentle, but there was a slight hedge of worry to it. Claude didn't work with Blair, but he saw him often enough around the office to be able to read his expression by now.

"Thank you," Blair said. "I'm glad to see you. I wasn't sure you'd come."

"I wouldn't have missed it for anything."

Edgar snorted. "Weren't you the one who was whining in the car just minutes ago?" he asked as he gave his son a one-arm sideway hug.

"You heard that wrong," Claude said.

Edgar laughed. "I doubt I'd be able to confuse your voice with anyone else's, but fine. We'll act as if you're thrilled to be here."

"I *am* happy to be here." And that wasn't a lie. He loved Edgar's family, and he enjoyed spending time with them. He just couldn't help that he felt out of place when he did. No matter how much he loved Edgar, he wasn't one of them.

Edgar and Blair looked at each other, and now, Claude was *sure* something was wrong.

"Before you go in, we have something to tell you," Blair said.

"What is it?" Claude couldn't imagine what the two wanted to talk to him about. If it was work, Edgar would have said something at the office. The fact that Blair was here, too, didn't bode well. "Are you about to tell me I'm fired?"

Blair gaped while Edgar reached out and lightly slapped the back of Claude's head. "How can you say something that stupid?"

Claude glared at him. "What? It's a legitimate question.

Both you and Blair are looking at me as if you expect me to blow up."

"We do, but not because we're firing you," Blair said. "I suppose we just have to come out and tell you. Wasting time isn't going to help."

"I hate it when people are cryptic. Just come out with whatever it is." The sooner they did, the sooner Claude could start dealing with it.

"It's something about our family and Jack's," Blair explained. "Something you need to know before you go in. My father and I should have told you long ago, but we didn't want to freak you out."

Claude still didn't understand what was happening.

"We're shifters," Edgar blurted out.

Claude blinked at him. "I'm sorry?"

Edgar waved. "Shifters. You know, people who can turn into animals."

Claude burst out laughing. "I didn't know you could be so funny. Really, though. What's going on? You don't have to lie to me to make me feel better." He wasn't entirely convinced that they weren't trying to fire him.

"I'm not lying," Edgar said. His expression was serious. "I've wanted to tell you this for a long time, but I didn't know how. I didn't want to lose you. I'm telling you now because Jack has a young niece. She doesn't understand that sometimes she shouldn't shift. We didn't want her to do that in front of you and freak you out, so Blair and I decided to tell you all of this before we went into the house."

Claude shook his head. "This can't be right. You expect me to believe that the two of you and Jack's entire family are werewolves?"

"Not wolves," Blair said.

He grabbed Claude's hand and pulled him toward the house. Claude followed because what else could he do?

They stepped into the house, and Blair closed the door. Then he turned to look at Claude. They were in the entrance, and Claude could hear the sound of people talking and laughing. It was intimidating, but not as much as the way Edgar and Blair stared at him.

Claude's eyes widened when Blair took off his sweater. "What are you doing?"

"Showing you that we're not lying."

"And you have to be naked to do that?"

Blair grinned. "It's easier. I can keep my jeans on if you're more comfortable."

"Please." Claude had no idea what was happening, but none of this felt right.

Blair handed his sweater to his father, then turned his attention back to Claude. He held his gaze, and for a second, nothing happened. Claude opened his mouth to tell Blair he could put his sweater back on because no matter how hot he was, he'd never be anything more than a brother, but before he could, Blair's body started to shrink.

Claude watched with wide eyes and a gaping mouth as Blair turned into a bird. He wasn't sure what kind of bird it was, but it was a bird of prey.

And that bird of prey was Blair.

Claude stumbled back.

What the actual fuck?

Andy opened his wings and ran after Melissa. She squawked and stood her ground instead of running away like he'd expected. She tried to mirror his position, opening her wings wide and staring at him.

Andy was impressed. She'd grown up fast in the past year, headed toward being a toddler rather than a baby, and it was incredible to watch. Watching Laurie with her was amazing, and while Andy wouldn't have believed it before, he had to admit that Laurie was doing a great job as a dad.

He lost Melissa's attention when three people entered the room from the entrance. Andy recognized Blair and his father, but the third man was a mystery, and he froze. Both Andy and Melissa were in their swan forms. It would be hard to explain having two swans in the living room, but he supposed Blair and Jack could say they were pets. The problem was that Melissa wasn't used to hiding the fact that she could turn into a swan. She shifted back and forth whenever she wanted, and today wasn't any different.

She screeched and rushed toward the newcomers. The man Andy didn't know was between Blair and his father, and he stared at her with wide eyes and stumbled back. She stopped in front of him, shifted to her human form, and held her arms out, clearly wanting to be picked up.

Melissa had never met a stranger she didn't like and didn't try to turn into family. The problem was that she'd shifted in front of this stranger, and now, everyone was in trouble.

"The kid was a swan," the man said.

Blair squeezed the man's shoulder. "That's what Dad and I were talking about. Almost everyone here is a shifter. We wanted you to know, because Melissa doesn't understand that she can't shift in front of people yet."

The man nodded. He was still staring at Melissa, but Andy wasn't worried that he'd hurt her. He wouldn't be able to try with so many people surrounding them.

He was cute, in a nerdy kind of way, which happened to be Andy's type. He was on the short side, with short auburn hair and glasses. He wore a pair of dress pants and a shirt, almost as if he was going to the office, but it suited him, and it was clear he was comfortable in them. The shirt clung to his upper body, showing Andy a hint of a stomach.

Andy's hands itched to touch him there. He wanted to

move closer, but swans could be intimidating. They had a reputation, and it wasn't wrong. Swans were fierce protectors, especially of their babies, but they were also assholes. Melissa was tiny still, but Andy was a full-fledged swan, and he didn't want to freak out the guy even more.

Melissa was still trying to get the guy to pick her up. Since it wasn't working, she shifted back and tried to fly up to the guy's arms.

Andy looked around. A few people were in the living room, but they were distracted. Leon was watching the scene, looking like it was the funniest thing he'd ever seen, and it was clear he wasn't about to step in.

Andy sighed. He supposed it would come down to him. He shifted and tried to ignore the fact that he was naked in front of a cute guy. His family was used to nudity, but the same couldn't be said for strangers, especially humans. He snatched Melissa out of the air the next time she tried to jump, clutched her to his chest, and quickly moved away. "Sorry about that," he said.

The guy stared at him and nodded, but he seemed dazed. Andy wasn't sure if it was because of the shifter thing or because he was naked.

"What's going on here?" Laurie asked as he walked in, holding Melissa's bottle. "Are the two of you still playing?"

"We're done," Andy said. "You can take her."

"I was going to even if you didn't tell me I could," he said, taking his daughter.

She instantly shifted back, ready for dinner.

Andy followed Laurie out of the living room. He was still naked, but he'd left his clothes in one of the guest rooms, so he needed to get there to get dressed. "Who's the guy with Blair and his father?" he asked.

Laurie shrugged. "No idea. You should ask Jack."

"As soon as I'm dressed."

Laurie chuckled. "That's probably a good idea. The guy looked like he was in shock, although I'm not sure if it's because you were naked or something else."

"Guys don't get shocked when I get naked," Andy grumbled.

It made Laurie laugh again. "Whatever you say."

Andy climbed the steps two by two, eager to get dressed. He wanted to find out who this guy was and why he was freaking out so badly. It was as if he hadn't known about shifters before, but then why was he here? He'd been with Blair and Blair's father, which meant he knew them. How was it possible that he hadn't been aware they were shifters until now?

The only way to find out what was happening was to ask, so Andy stormed into the guestroom, grabbed his clothes from the bed, and quickly put them on. He stopped by the bathroom to wash his hands and face, checked his hair, then headed downstairs.

He didn't know why he wanted to talk to this guy so much, but he expected to have to do so in front of the others. Instead, he found out he was lucky, because as he came down the stairs, he saw the guy standing there by himself in the entrance. He was staring out one of the windows that framed the front door, but he turned when he heard Andy. His eyes widened and he took a step back, which Andy decided meant he needed to keep his distance, too. The guy was terrified, and Andy didn't want him to be afraid of him.

He didn't want anyone to be afraid of him, but the strength of his feelings almost scared him. He also didn't understand what was happening, which didn't make things easier.

"Hi," he said, stopping at the bottom of the stairs.

Since the guy was by the front door, that kept enough distance between them so he wouldn't feel crowded, and if he needed to, he could leave. He wasn't trapped, which Andy suspected was important.

"You're not naked anymore," the guy said.

Andy barked out a laugh. He hadn't expected that. "I don't usually hang around naked, especially not in my brother's house."

"That's kind of a pity. You looked good naked." The guy snapped his mouth shut, and his cheeks turned bright red. "Sorry about that. I'm feeling a bit overwhelmed and don't know what I'm saying."

Andy smiled. He didn't want this guy to be afraid of him. "That's all right. I'm Andy, one of Jack's brothers."

The guy smiled. It was tense, but it was a smile. "Which one of the six are you?"

"Second to youngest. There's Laurie, then me, then Jack."

"I'm Claude, Edgar's personal assistant."

Andy knew Edgar was Blair's father, but he wasn't quite sure why the man's personal assistant was here. "Are the two of you close?"

"Very much so, or at least, I thought so until today. I could never have imagined he was keeping such a big secret from me."

Andy grimaced. So Claude hadn't known anything about shifters until today. "Well, I'm not sure how close the two of you are, although it seems the answer to that is very much so. But I can tell you that it's never easy to decide when you should tell someone about shifters. For one, you have to trust the other person completely. Things never end up well when people sell us out to the government because we're freaks of nature."

Claude frowned. "I'd never do that."

"I know."

"How? You just met me."

"But you wouldn't be here if Blair didn't trust you. He wouldn't have told you anything about shifters if he didn't, which means he knows you're not going to try to hurt us."

"I'm still freaked out."

"Who wouldn't be? I grew up knowing about shifters, obviously, but I can imagine it's not easy for you."

"It's not, and I have no idea how to deal with any of this."

"Slowly. You don't have to wrap your mind around all of it and what it means right away. Take some time to think about it. Ask as many questions as you need. Just remember that even though Edgar and Blair can turn into animals, it doesn't mean they're not the same people you knew before."

For some reason, it was important for Andy that Claude remembered that. He didn't want Claude to think he was nothing more than an animal. He wanted Claude to see him for the man he was, even though none of it made sense.

Andy's advice sounded good. There was no way Claude could wrap his mind around what he'd just found out in just a few hours or even a few days. Once he managed to accept that shifters were real and not something that existed only in books and movies, he'd have so many questions for Edgar, and he expected an answer to all of them. Edgar owed it to him after keeping this a secret for so long.

But that wouldn't happen today. Today, Claude was trying to wrap his mind around the fact that he was about to have dinner with a bunch of people who could turn into animals.

"Wait, you were a swan," he said.

Andy nodded. "Yes. My mother is a swan shifter, and we all took after her."

"So it's genetic? I mean, the animal you can turn into isn't random?"

"Not at all. Like I said, my mother is a swan shifter, so all of us are. Melissa is Laurie's daughter, so she's a swan shifter, too."

Claude nodded. "So I guess that Blair is whatever kind of bird Edgar can turn into."

"They're osprey shifters."

Claude had no idea what that was. "Is it only birds?"

Andy leaned against the railing. He looked at ease here, which made sense since his brother lived in this house. Claude wished he could feel the same way, but right now, it wouldn't take much to send him running out of the house screaming his head off.

"Nope. Laurie's mate, Alexis, is a wolf shifter, while Peter is a hedgehog shifter. He's my brother Sean's mate."

Unfortunately, Andy's answer meant that Claude had even more questions now. "Mate?"

"Do you read romance novels?"

The question startled a smile out of Claude. "Why? Do I look like I do?"

Andy shrugged. "I don't know. But if you've read romance novels, you'd know what mates are. They're soulmates. We only have one, and we spend the rest of our lives with them when we meet them."

"So like a husband?"

Andy wiggled his hand this way and that. "More or less. It's what we call each other out in public with humans around, but the mate bond is deeper than a bond between two husbands. We'll never get a divorce or anything like that. Your mate is perfect for you, and when you meet them, that's it. My parents have been together since they met each other. Blair's parents, too. And all my brothers will be with their mates for the rest of their lives."

Claude leaned against the front door. He needed it because he felt like he might be about to faint.

Andy took a step forward, a frown on his face, but he quickly stopped.

Claude was glad because he wasn't sure how he'd have

reacted if Andy had tried touching him. He didn't think Andy or anyone else here wanted to hurt him, but there was a part of his brain that was telling him to run.

They weren't natural. People who could turn into animals? Claude had never heard anything like that beyond the romance novels Andy believed he read.

He was right.

Claude did know what mates were. He'd read many books where they were a thing, and he hadn't needed Andy's explanation, although it was nice to have confirmation from a real-life shifter.

"You should probably go home," Andy whispered.

Claude blinked. "I'm sorry?"

"You look like you're about to faint. I guess if you just found out about shifters, you need some time to process everything. Maybe you could come back for the family dinner next week? I want to show you that shifters aren't dangerous, but I don't think that's going to happen tonight."

"I came with Edgar."

"That's not a problem. I'll call you a taxi or something."

"I'll do it." Claude could afford a ride back to the city, even though it would be an hour's drive. He didn't want Andy to pay for him, especially since he was the one freaking out and needing time.

Andy watched him as he took out his phone and used his app. It would take ten minutes for the car to arrive, but Claude wasn't sure he could wait in the house. He needed out, and he needed it now.

But before he left, he had something to say. "Thank you."

"What are you thanking me for?" Andy asked.

"Trying to help me. There's nothing you can do to make it easier for me to accept all of this, but you tried, and I think you're right. Once I have some time to think about this, I'll feel better."

"And you'll come back for the family dinner?"

Claude should say no. He didn't belong here, especially without Edgar. But he was surprised to realize he didn't *want* to say no. He wanted to find out more about shifters and Andy in particular, and the only way to get that was to come back for family dinner. "Your family won't mind?"

"They'll love to have you. My mother feeds anyone who ends up at her table, so she'll be delighted."

That was a far cry from Claude's mother. "I'll come back, then. Thank you."

Claude's jacket was in the entrance, so he grabbed it and put it on. He was sorry to leave but needed to do it for his sanity. Hopefully, Edgar would understand.

Andy stayed in the entrance as Claude stepped out and closed the door. Claude took a deep breath, enjoying the feeling of cold air on his skin.

But of course, things couldn't go easily. He was waiting for the car at the end of the driveway when he heard the front door open. He turned to see Edgar walk out of the house. He sighed, because he'd known Edgar would have something to say about him sneaking out.

"What are you doing out here?" Edgar asked.

"Waiting for a car. I'm going home."

"Why? You don't have to be afraid of any of us. I promise you that no one here will hurt you. Melissa might bite you, but she's just a kid."

Claude shook his head. "It's not that. I know you wouldn't hurt me. I'm just—it's a lot, you know?"

Edgar pushed his hands into his pockets. "I'm sorry. I should have told you all of this a long time ago."

Claude had been angry that Edgar hadn't earlier, but he understood better after his conversation with Andy. "I'm not angry at you. I'm just in shock."

"So you're not going to quit your job and avoid me?"

Claude stared at Edgar for a second. He loved the man as much as he would have loved his father if he'd known him. He couldn't imagine his life without Edgar, job or no job.

On instinct, he pulled Edgar into a hug. Edgar jerked back, clearly surprised, but he leaned in after a few seconds. They hugged for a moment, and Claude hoped it was enough to tell Edgar that no, he wasn't going to quit his job.

"You're in my life to stay," Claude said when he stepped away. "Whether you like it or not."

Edgar chuckled. It sounded slightly watery, and Claude didn't think he'd be able to stand it if Edgar started crying. He was an ugly crier and didn't want anyone to see him like that.

"I very much want you in my life," Edgar said.

"Then this isn't going to change anything. Just give me some time, all right?"

Edgar nodded. "I'll see you tomorrow at the office?"

"You will." Because Edgar would be lost without Claude, and Claude didn't want to put too much distance between them. Even after what he'd found out tonight, Edgar was his family, along with Blair and Mathilde. That wouldn't change, no matter what he learned about them.

As long as they weren't serial killers, anyway.

CHAPTER TWO

There was a bounce in Andy's steps as he walked into his parents' house. Usually, he and Jack arrived together, but that wasn't the case anymore. It felt weird, but for once, Andy wasn't sad.

And he knew exactly why.

The entire week, he'd been thinking about Claude. He still remembered the man's wary and worried expression, and he wanted to see if Claude had gotten over his shock. Hopefully, the answer to that would be yes. It would be awful for him to have dinner with the family if he was afraid of shifters.

That wasn't the only reason Andy wanted Claude to be okay with shifters. He'd barely talked to Claude, but he could admit, at least to himself, that he had a crush on the man. It was ridiculous, and Andy wasn't a teenager anymore, but liking Claude made him happier than usual. He hadn't obsessed over everything changing and his brother living with his mate now in days, and he took that as a win. It would take time for Andy to get used to his new life without his brother's permanent presence by his side, but he could do it. He was an adult, and didn't need Jack to hold his hand.

Andy made a beeline for the kitchen because he knew that was where he'd find his mother, and a visit home couldn't start without saying hello to her and his dad. Sure enough, she was in front of the stove, and he came up behind her and kissed her cheek. She squeaked and waved her wooden spoon at him, her eyes narrow even though Andy knew she wasn't angry.

"Don't do that."

Andy grinned. "I like to surprise you."

"Well, I don't like being surprised when cooking. I could have messed up everything."

"You could never mess up food. You're too good at cooking."

His mother's cheeks flushed and she turned back. "There's no need to butter me up." She eyed him sideways. "You look happy today."

Andy leaned his hip against the counter and crossed his arms over his chest. "That's because I am."

"Well, it's good to see. I was worried about you last week."

Andy felt guilty. His mother shouldn't have to worry about him. Almost all of her sons had met their mates and were happy. Laurie even had a daughter. She should be focused on them and their happiness rather than on Andy's moping. He supposed it made sense that she'd been worried about him, though. She didn't have to worry about the others anymore, at least not when it came to their love lives and their happiness. Andy was the odd brother out, but something told him that maybe, it wouldn't be for long.

"You have nothing to worry about," he said as he leaned closer and kissed his mom on the cheek again. "I'm fine. I'm happy for Jack and everyone else, and I'm sure my time will come eventually."

His mom squinted. "Have you met someone?"

Andy wasn't sure how to answer that. He had no idea whether or not there could be something between him and Claude, and he didn't want his mother to get her hopes up before he knew if that was the case. "I don't know. Possibly." Because if he didn't give her at least this, she'd hound him until he did.

Her smile lit up the kitchen. "Really? Who is he? Where did you meet him? When am I meeting him?"

Andy laughed. His mother could be nosy, but it was because she cared about them. She wanted all of them to be happy, and she only intervened when that wasn't the case, or at least, she tried to limit herself to those situations. She wanted her babies to be safe, which meant meeting their significant others. She wasn't pushy or invasive, but she still ensured they were safe.

"I'm not sure of anything right now," he told her. "We met recently, and we barely talked, but I like him, and I hope to see him again soon. I promise I'll tell you what's happening once I'm sure there's something there. As far as I know, it could be only wishful thinking."

"Well, if he doesn't ask you out or say yes when you do, he's a fool. You're a catch."

It warmed Andy's heart to hear his mother talk that way. "You have to say that. I'm your son."

"So? I'd be the first to admit that Laurie was hard to deal with. Alexis had more patience than I would have had in his place. You, though, are a sweetheart. It's odd that you weren't one of the first to meet your mate."

Andy didn't want to think about that right now. "I will eventually, and if I don't, it doesn't mean I can't be with someone else."

"Exactly. Don't obsess over the mate thing. I know most shifters want to meet their mate because they think it's a guarantee of happiness, but it's not. Being in any kind of relationship is hard work."

Andy was aware of that, but he wanted what his mother and father had. They'd been together forever, and they were still as much in love as they'd been those first days, or at least, he imagined they were. Obviously, he hadn't known them back then, but for as long as he could remember, they'd been happy together.

Andy wanted someone to be happy with that way.

His mother opened one of the cupboards and took a pile of plates from it. "Now go help your brother set the table. He hasn't come back to the kitchen in a while, which tells me he's probably distracted."

Andy didn't ask which brother she was talking about. He'd find out soon enough. He took the plates and headed to the dining room, grinning when he found Jack and Blair kissing. Jack was leaning against the wall, his arms wrapped around Blair's neck. He was still holding a bunch of napkins in one of his hands.

Andy cleared his throat loudly, chuckling when Blair and Jack jumped apart. Jack glared, but Andy was used to his brother. "Now I know why you didn't go back to the kitchen," he said as he put the plates on the table.

Jack groaned. "The table."

"Exactly. Mom sent me to help you since you're not doing a good job on your own."

Blair chuckled. "We were distracted."

Andy hesitated. A question burned on his lips, but he wasn't sure it would be the best thing to ask it. Blair was the only one who could answer, so Andy decided to go with it. "Do you know if Claude is coming?"

He could feel both Blair and Jack staring at him, but he focused on putting down the plates in the best spot so they would be easily available to everyone.

"Why are you asking?" Jack asked.

"None of your business."

"Isn't it? I like to know when my brother has a crush."

Andy hoped he wasn't blushing. "I don't have a crush. I barely know the guy, but I was worried about him last week." He glared at Blair. "That probably wasn't the best way to tell him about us."

Blair grimaced. "I agree. I was surprised my father had never told him, but maybe I shouldn't have been. My father cares a lot about him, and he was afraid Claude would leave the job and him behind if he found out."

"He hasn't?"

"No. I don't see Claude often because he works for my father, not with me, but I've seen him around the office this week. And yes, he's coming for dinner along with my parents."

Andy beamed. He couldn't help it. He was eager to see Claude again, to find out if Claude had wrapped his mind around shifters being real and if maybe there could be something between them.

Even though he and Claude barely had time to talk last week, Andy liked him. He'd decided over the past week that he wouldn't wait for his mate—he didn't know if he'd ever meet him, and he wanted to be happy, even if it wasn't with the man destined to be with him.

So he was planning on asking Claude out if Claude had gotten over his fear. He had no idea if it could become something, but he was ready to find out, and he couldn't wait. Claude might not be his mate, but that didn't mean he and Andy couldn't have what all of Andy's brothers had—someone to love and who loved them, someone to share their lives with, someone to be happy with.

Claude kept bouncing his knee and wondering if he should have come with his own car. He could have used it last week instead of paying his weight in money to the guy who'd driven him home, but Edgar had been offended when he'd suggested coming separately. He hadn't said much, but he'd been walking on eggshells around Claude the entire week.

Claude knew why. Edgar was afraid of losing him, and no matter how many times Claude told him he wasn't going anywhere, his boss and friend was worried.

Claude didn't blame him. He'd been obsessing over the news that shifters were real the entire week, and he still didn't know what to think about it. He'd decided to accept it as a fact of life, and after that, it had been slightly easier. Besides, Edgar wasn't any different. The fact that he could turn into a huge ass bird didn't change the person he was. He was still gentle, caring, fierce, and a good friend.

That didn't mean Claude wasn't worried about how dinner would go. He hadn't made the best impression last week, leaving five minutes after he'd arrived at Blair's birthday party. He'd been building up the courage to apologize, something he wouldn't have needed to do before finding out about shifters. He wasn't afraid of Blair, Edgar, and the others, but even though they hadn't changed as people, it was still odd because Claude saw them differently.

It wasn't a bad thing. It was just weird, and he hoped that in time, he'd manage to forget they weren't entirely human.

"I couldn't find the Donovan folder this morning," Edgar suddenly said.

Claude scowled at him in the rearview mirror. "That's because I hid it. What were you doing, trying to find the folder this morning when it's Sunday?"

"I just wanted to go over a few things. Where did you hide it?"

"Somewhere you won't think of finding it. I'm not giving it to you until tomorrow at the office."

"But why? I can work during the weekend. I'm the boss, so I get to decide."

Claude snorted. "From where I'm sitting, Mathilde is the boss, and she told you to stop working during the weekends."

Edgar quickly glanced at his wife—his *mate*—and she smiled at him. "It won't kill you not to work for two days," she said.

"But I was bored this morning." There was a whine in

25

Edgar's voice.

"Then you should have found something to amuse your-self that wasn't work."

Claude grinned. He loved spending time with them and watching them together. It was so obvious that they loved each other, and now he understood better how they could still be happy after all these years. Edgar had told him they were mates, and from what Andy had said, mates were meant to be together forever.

For some reason, Claude couldn't stop thinking about Andy the entire week. He was the main reason Claude was going back tonight. He wanted to thank Andy, but that wasn't the only thing he wanted to do to him.

Claude's cheeks heated, and he looked out the window. He hadn't asked Andy if he had a mate. If he remembered correctly, Andy had mentioned that several of his brothers were in a relationship with their mates, but he'd never said anything about himself. That had made Claude curious, but there was more to it than curiosity, and he didn't understand it. Why did he want to get to know Andy so badly? As far as Claude knew, Andy was just a guy. Sure, he could turn into a black swan, and it was impressive, just like he looked impressive naked, but there was nothing else to it.

Right?

Claude wasn't one to believe in insta-love. Insta-lust, possibly, but that wasn't the kind of guy he was. It wasn't like he wanted to have sex with Andy, though.

Well, of course, he did. He'd seen Andy naked, but even more, Andy had been kind and gentle, and Claude liked that. Maybe it was because Claude wasn't one who wanted sex for sex's sake, but he wanted to get to know Andy. He also wanted to end up in bed with him, but he didn't want things to end there.

He bit his lower lip. He had to stop thinking this way.

Relationships never worked, and he'd promised himself he'd stay away from men after his last messy breakup. That included Andy, unfortunately.

"Is everything ready for the party?" Edgar asked, cutting through Claude's thoughts.

Claude blinked. "I'm sorry?"

"The office party. Is everything ready for it?"

The thought almost made Claude cringe. "Of course."

Edgar looked at him from the rearview mirror. "I expect you to be there."

"There's no reason for me to be. I'm just a personal assistant, and you're not supposed to work during the party."

"We both know that's not how this works. It's a *work* party, so people will be working, networking at the very least." Edgar sighed. "I understand why you don't want to be there. We can't avoid inviting Michael, but you can't hide from him. You can't let him win."

"I'm not letting him win or do anything else. I just don't want to see him. I don't want to deal with him or any of the problems that come with him."

"But it's work. Surely, you won't shy away from a work event just because of Michael. He expects you to run from him and not to be there. Can you imagine how smug he'll be when he realizes you're not there?"

Claude *really* didn't want to see Michael again. If he had a choice, he'd never see Michael again in his entire life. Unfortunately, Edgar was right. Michael would be there during the party, and Claude couldn't avoid going because it was a work thing. Michael would instantly know that Claude wasn't there because of him if he wasn't present, and he'd be victorious. After what had happened between them, Claude wanted Michael to feel like the lowest of the low, not like he'd won.

Besides, not everything had to do with Michael. Claude took his job seriously, so he couldn't avoid attending this party.

"What Michael did was awful," Mathilde said softly. "But Edgar is right. You can't let him win." She made a disgusted sound. "I should have torn Michael's balls off the last time I had him in front of me."

Claude was startled by her words, but he shouldn't be. He was closest to Edgar, but the entire family had welcomed him as if he were one of them. He regularly met Edgar and Mathilde for lunch or dinner, and while he saw Blair less often, especially now that he'd moved in with Jack, Lisa always had a smile for him. It was a bit awkward because Claude wasn't part of their family, but they made him feel like he was. He was never quite sure how to deal with it, but it was good to have them in his life, especially considering his mother.

He took out his phone and opened the string of texts he'd exchanged with his mother. She wasn't a bad mother. She regularly contacted him, asking him how he was and if he needed anything. She cared about him, but she couldn't get over her hatred of relationships and general negative view of life.

Claude stopped on the messages she'd sent him when he'd told her he'd broken up with Michael.

That was the best thing you could do. Relationships never work, no matter how perfect the guy seems to be.

You'll be better off on your own. Trust me. I have experience when it comes to that.

He didn't deserve you. None of them deserve you.

Claude sighed. Being with Michael had been his last attempt to show his mother that she was wrong. He'd thought she was letting her failed relationships sully the way she saw love, but clearly, she hadn't been wrong. Maybe some people weren't made to be in relationships. If that was the case, neither Claude nor his mother were. His mom always said she was better on her own, but Claude wasn't sure that was the case for himself. Still, since relationships didn't work for them, it would be better to stay away from guys.

For some reason, when he thought about staying away from guys, his chest squeezed because he didn't want to stay away from Andy. Andy was a guy, and he'd seemed nice.

But Michael had been nice in the beginning, too. Then he'd shown his true colors. Claude couldn't trust anyone—not Michael, not Andy.

But why did he so desperately want Andy to be one of the good guys his mother insisted didn't exist?

Andy felt like he was about to jump out of his skin by the time he heard a car stop in the driveway. Every time before, it had been one of his brothers. Not all of them were there, but it wouldn't be a family dinner if most hadn't been. This time, though, it wasn't one of Andy's brothers. This time, it was Blair's parents, along with Claude.

Andy spied on them through the living room window. He'd placed himself behind the curtain so Claude wouldn't notice him, and while he felt like an idiot, he wanted to see Claude and try to understand if he was more relaxed this week.

"What are you doing?" Jack suddenly asked from behind Andy.

Andy jumped and turned to glare at his brother. "Why did you sneak up behind me?"

"I wanted to see what was happening. Who are we spying on?" He peeked out the window, his eyes widening when he saw who it was. "Why didn't you tell me Blair's parents were here?"

"They just arrived," Andy grumbled.

He could see Jack was nervous. Even though he and Blair were destined to be together, Jack and Blair's parents had had a rocky first meeting. They'd assumed he'd be moving in with

Blair in the city, and Jack had freaked out and run back home. He'd known he wouldn't be able to live there long term, away from their family and everything he'd known all his life. Luckily for him, Blair had agreed and bought them a house in town.

"How are things going with them?" Andy asked.

Jack shrugged. "As well as they can. I'm not about to become their best friend, but they're respectful and don't have anything to say against my relationship with Blair."

"They seem like good people."

"They are. They're different from us, but it doesn't make them bad people. Just different."

Andy couldn't disagree. Blair and his parents were rich, and while Andy and his family had never wanted for anything, they lived different lives. It was good to see that Blair and Jack were making it work. It gave Andy hope that even though he and Claude led different lives in different cities, they'd find a way to make things work between them.

That was if Claude wanted things to work between them. So far, it was a one-way thing, but he had to remember that didn't mean Claude wasn't interested in him. Andy just needed to be careful and not overwhelm him.

He heard his mother open the door and welcome Blair's parents and Claude in. Then chaos descended on the house.

Tonight, Andy's mother had decided to make a buffet-style dinner. It took them almost fifteen minutes to bring all the food from the kitchen to the dining room. They'd pushed the dining table against the wall, and there were enough plates for everyone to grab one and fill it. They'd lined the walls with chairs so everyone could sit down wherever they wanted and chat with whoever they sat next to. They usually only did this during Christmas and other family celebrations, and it was a bit odd to see strangers right in the middle of it. It wasn't a bad thing, though. Their family was expanding, including mates and their parents, and hopefully, children.

Andy and Jack were waiting for their turn at the table when Jack elbowed Andy in the ribs. "He's quiet," he murmured.

Andy looked around, finding Claude standing by the dining-room door. Blair's parents, on the other hand, felt like they were already part of the family. They were right in the middle of it, filling their plates and talking to people.

"Is he always like that?" Andy asked.

"I don't know him that well. He's close to Edgar, but I don't work with them, so I haven't had the opportunity to get to know him. Why don't you go talk to him?"

"I will."

"Maybe make sure he eats something. He's going to need it if you're going to ask him out."

Andy glared at his brother. "Shut up." He didn't want anyone to hear anything about this before he had the opportunity to talk to Claude.

"What? You're the only one still single. We're all invested in your happiness."

There was teasing in Jack's voice, but Andy knew he was telling the truth. His brothers all wanted Andy to be happy, and they were rooting for him, even though most of them didn't know he had a crush on Claude. Jack wasn't one to spread gossip, but eventually the others would catch up. Then Andy would have to answer a thousand questions, and he hoped he'd have answers by then.

"We have an announcement," Leon suddenly said. He stood in the middle of the dining room, looking delighted.

Andy wasn't sure that was a good thing, but like everyone else, he turned his full attention to him and focused on whatever he was about to say.

Leon looked around, found Hugh, and held his hand out. Hugh hated being the center of attention, so it said a lot that he didn't hesitate to take Leon's hand and stand with him in the spotlight.

Leon looked around, and once he was sure he had everyone's attention, he nodded to himself. "Hugh and I have decided to expand our family. We've been looking into adoption, and we were contacted this morning. We're going to be parents."

For a moment, no one said anything. Then the room exploded. Every single member of the family made their way toward Hugh and Leon.

Andy wasn't any different. He grabbed his brother and hugged him, slapping his back. "I'm so happy for you."

Hugh hugged him back. "Thank you. We weren't sure it would come through, but it's a shifter woman. She wants her child to be adopted by shifters, so that made it easier."

"That's great."

Andy had a lot of questions, but he realized everyone did. Hugh looked overwhelmed, so Andy stepped away and decided to wait to ask them. He headed toward the table, ready to finally eat, when he noticed Claude was filling his plate. He wasn't celebrating with the others, but that made sense since he wasn't part of their family yet. He didn't know Hugh and Leon, so he couldn't be as happy as everyone else about their announcement.

Andy watched Claude as he filled his plate, then looked around. The living room was still too noisy, so Andy wasn't surprised to see him head toward the kitchen. He quickly filled his plate, then went after Claude.

The kitchen was empty, so Andy pushed open the back door. He peeked out, smiling when he saw Claude was sitting on the porch swing. Claude turned wide eyes to him, and Andy stepped out and closed the door behind himself. "Do you mind if I eat here with you?" he asked.

"Of course not. This is your house, and you can do whatever you want."

"It's not my house. My parents live here, but I don't. If you don't want me to eat with you, just tell me, and I'll go back inside."

Claude didn't even hesitate before he shook his head. "You can stay. I don't mind."

Andy was relieved. They hadn't had an opportunity to talk yet, so he didn't know if Claude was still spooked about the shifters thing. He moved slowly, settling next to Claude on the porch swing.

They'd never been so close. Last week in the entrance, Andy had kept his distance because he hadn't wanted Claude to feel crowded. There was no avoiding leaning against him tonight, and Andy took a deep breath.

That was when Claude's scent hit him. Andy's mouth dropped open. How had he not noticed this last week? How had he not realized Claude was his mate the first time they'd met?

And now that he had realized it, what was he supposed to do with the knowledge? He wanted to blurt everything out, but from the way Claude stared at him, he could tell Claude was still wary.

No, the best thing would be to keep it to himself, at least for a bit. He needed to know how Claude felt about shifters before he could tell him they were destined to be together.

Claude wasn't sure what to think of Andy. He'd been telling himself that maybe Andy wasn't as great as he remembered, but that wasn't true. He'd asked permission to sit next to Claude, and instead of starting to talk right away, he was eating quietly. He kept peeking at Claude, almost as if he wanted to ask him a question, but so far, he hadn't, and it made Claude feel nervous.

What did Andy want from him? Was he as fascinated with

Claude as Claude was with him?

Claude tried to push those thoughts away. He was done with relationships and men. He was happy enough in his life that he didn't need a guy to complete it, and that was that.

Or at least, that was what he was trying to convince himself of. But he wasn't his mother, who'd been single for years. He'd always wanted love, even when he could see it didn't work for him. He was terrified of getting his heart broken again, so he'd decided that the best thing to do would be to keep Andy at arm's length.

But thinking about Andy and relationships made Claude think of Michael. He still didn't understand what he'd seen in the asshole, but he dreaded seeing him at the party. He knew Michael wouldn't come alone. He'd have a pretty twink on his arm and flaunt it in Claude's face. He'd be smug that Claude was on by himself. He'd told Claude that he would never find anyone better than him when he tried to convince Claude to stay with him, which hadn't worked as well as he'd expected.

Claude couldn't stand the thought of Michael being happy to see him unattached, which was the only explanation he could think of for the words that came out of his mouth. "Want to be my fake boyfriend?"

The silence that met his question was absolute. Claude had to resist the urge to run and hide in the house until Mathilde and Edgar were ready to leave. Hell, he might get a cab this time, too.

He started getting to his feet, but Andy's hand shot forward and wrapped around his wrist. They stayed frozen for a second, and Claude was afraid to look at Andy. He'd been nothing but nice, but this was no doubt too much.

"I'm sorry," Claude said. "I didn't mean to say that."

"I don't think you would have said it if you hadn't meant to say it," Andy commented. "You don't have to leave. We were eating."

"I was going to run because that was so embarrassing."

Andy chuckled and let go of Claude. "I'm not going to force you to stay, but you don't have to leave if you don't want to. Besides, I want to know more about why you need me to be your fake boyfriend."

Claude sat down. He was relieved Andy wasn't angry, but he still thought this was the worst idea he could ever have had. He didn't want to explain, but he felt Andy deserved to know what was happening.

"So, why did you ask me that?" Andy asked when they started eating again.

Claude wasn't hungry anymore, but he forced himself to put food in his mouth. It was good. "We have a work party next week," he explained. "I have to be there because it's work, but my ex will be there, too. He's, well, I'm pretty sure he has someone new in his life, and I didn't want to be alone to face him. It was a stupid idea."

"I don't think it was stupid. I don't know what happened, but he hurt you, right?"

Claude snorted. That Michael had hurt him was an understatement. Claude had been in love with him, had trusted him, and Michael had stomped on that trust. "He did. He kept telling me that he wanted to marry me, and we moved in together, probably too fast. My mother cautioned me about it, but I didn't listen to her. I always thought she was too negative about relationships because hers failed. Maybe she was right."

"Relationships don't have to end badly. I mean, look at my brothers."

"I guess. Relationships always end badly for my mother and me, though, so she was probably right. Michael and I moved in together, and I was happy, at least until I came home early from work and found him fucking another guy in our bed."

It was so cliché that Claude almost couldn't believe it when he saw it. He'd stared until the twink Michael was fucking noticed him and screeched. Then he'd turned around and left the apartment. When he'd gone back a few hours later, Michael was alone. Claude hadn't known how to feel or what to say, but Michael hadn't let him say a word. He'd told Claude that the other guy didn't mean anything and that it was Claude's fault for not giving Michael sex anytime he wanted it.

Claude had packed up his things that evening, and he'd never gone back. What had happened wasn't his fault, and he would never allow anyone to convince him otherwise.

"I'm sorry," Andy murmured.

"You have nothing to be sorry about. You weren't the one who betrayed me. Michael is one of Edgar's clients, so we can't avoid inviting him to the party. He was pissed when I left him and tried to convince me that the other guy didn't matter, but I wouldn't have any of it. He told me I'd regret dumping him, and I'm sure he expects me to be sad and mopey at the party. I don't regret dumping him, but I also don't want him to be happy because I'm alone."

"So you want me to be your fake boyfriend."

"I know it was a stupid idea. I should just stand up to him and tell him to fuck off."

"I don't think it was stupid, and I'll do it."

Claude gaped. "Why?"

"Why not? You need help, and it's not like I have a boyfriend who would take offense."

"But we don't know each other. Why would you do that for someone you don't know?"

"You're family."

"I'm not."

"But you are. We might not be blood related, but we don't

need to be for me to care about you and want to help you. Please, let me do this for you. You deserve to have someone stand by your side when you face that asshole. I'll be happy to be that someone and tell him to fuck off if he even looks your way."

Claude could continue saying no, but he didn't want to. Andy would be perfect as his fake boyfriend. Besides, it would be a fake relationship, so Claude wouldn't have to worry about putting his heart on the line. "All right. But please, let me know if you don't feel up for it at any time. I won't be angry, but I want to be prepared."

Andy put his plate on the porch railing and took his phone out of his jeans pocket. "I won't change my mind. Now, give me your number. You'll have to send me all the details of this party, and I need to know how I have to dress. Is it something posh?"

Claude wasn't sure if he was lucky or not to have Andy offer himself like that. He wanted to spend more time with Andy, but he needed to remember there couldn't be anything between them. He was done with relationships, and no matter how nice Andy was, Claude couldn't trust him.

But he and Andy would have to behave as if they were together, at least at the party. That meant they needed to get to know each other and put together the story of how they'd gotten together. Claude shouldn't feel as thrilled as he did at the thought of spending more time talking to Andy, but he decided that was a problem he'd face after the party. Right now, he just wanted to focus on Andy and their fake relationship, so that was what he'd do.

Everything else would be a problem for future Claude.

CHAPTER THREE

When Andy woke up the next day, Claude was the first thing that came to mind.

He still couldn't believe he'd met his mate. No matter how many times he thought about it, no matter how he turned that around in his mind, he couldn't understand it.

He'd met his mate.

He stared at the ceiling as he thought about the evening before. He and Claude had spent most of it on the porch, talking. After Claude told him about his ex, Andy had wanted nothing more than to tell him they were mates, but he hadn't. It was clear Claude was wary of relationships and guys, and Andy didn't blame him. He hoped that knowing Andy was his mate would mean Claude saw him differently, but he couldn't be sure, and it made him nervous.

Just for that, he kind of wanted to kill Michael. He would never hurt anyone, not even that douchebag, so he'd decided that he'd show Michael just how desirable and lovable Claude was instead. Michael hadn't been able to see that, and really, it was Andy's win.

Now that he'd met Claude, he'd do everything he could to keep him in his life and happy. Michael had been too selfish to do that, but Andy couldn't say he was sorry. Things would have been awkward if Claude had still been dating Michael when they met.

But he wasn't. Instead, he'd gotten his heart broken, and Andy wasn't sure he could help him put it back together. He wanted Claude to love him and for them to be together, but he understood why Claude might be opposed to that.

Andy would have to take things slow and be careful.

He rolled to his side and grabbed his phone from the nightstand. His alarm was about to go off, so he hopped out of bed and headed to the bathroom. There was no message from Claude, but it was too early for him to be texting anyone, let alone a guy he barely knew.

Andy used the bathroom, washed up, and dressed for work. He tried to stop obsessing over Claude and ignore his phone during the day, but he'd never had such a hard time doing so. His boss kept staring at him, clearly having noticed Andy was distracted, but Andy snuck out during lunchtime before Tim could start asking questions. He wasn't up to answering them, especially when he couldn't be a hundred percent honest. As long as he didn't hurt himself while working on a car because he was distracted, it wasn't his boss's business to know about Claude. Tim was a friend, but for now, there was nothing for him to know.

Andy walked down the street, headed to the coffee shop so he could grab a sandwich. As he did so, he took out his phone, grinning when he saw he finally had a text from Claude. It wasn't much, just the details of the party and instructions on what Andy should wear, but it made everything more real.

The party was this weekend. That meant that Andy would see Claude again soon, and he was both ecstatic and extremely nervous. He needed to talk to someone, possibly someone who knew Claude, and the first person that came to mind was Blair.

So after work—and after avoiding his boss for the rest of the day—that was where Andy headed. He was relieved to see the lights were on when he got there and not one bit surprised when Blair opened the door when he knocked. Jack sometimes stayed late at work, but Blair mostly worked from home these days.

Blair looked surprised to see him there. "Andy. Were we expecting you for dinner?"

Andy grinned. "You weren't. This is an impromptu visit, and if you don't have enough food for me, I can leave when it's time for you to eat."

"You can stay as long as you like spaghetti."

"I happen to love spaghetti." And pasta in general. Carbs were life, as far as Andy was concerned.

"Jack is upstairs showering." Blair closed the door behind Andy and gestured toward the kitchen. "Come on. You can sit down while you wait for him."

"I'm not bothering you, right?" It was still weird to make sure of that.

Before, when Andy had wanted to talk to Jack, he could just knock on his bedroom door and walk in. Jack never brought anyone home, so Andy always knew he'd find him alone. But Jack wasn't alone anymore. He shared his life and his home with his mate, which meant that if Blair wanted Andy to leave, Andy would have to. He wouldn't blame Blair for wanting some privacy. He'd be the first to admit he was having a hard time letting go of his brother, and he was glad Blair didn't seem to care that they spent a lot of time together. Andy didn't visit every day, but he and Jack talked every evening on the phone.

"It's a good thing I'm getting used to having you around," Blair said as he went to the stove to peek into one of the pots there. "I've been cooking way too much for two people, which considering how much your brother can eat, is a lot."

"You don't have to keep cooking for me, you know."

"I don't mind. I like making Jack happy, and he's happy when he spends time with you." He hesitated. "I understand how close you are and that it's odd for both of you to spend so much time apart. I want to make this transition as easy as possible."

Andy shouldn't have been surprised. Blair wanted Jack to be happy as much as he did. It was one thing they had in common — wanting Jack's happiness.

The sound of a herd of elephants coming down the steps made both Andy and Blair turn. Blair seemed amused and had a fond expression that changed to a smile when Jack burst into the kitchen.

"I thought I'd heard Andy," he said, coming toward the counter. He kissed Blair's cheek, then slapped Andy's back. "What are you doing here? Freeloading?"

"I'll have you know that I asked Blair if he wanted me to leave before dinner. He's the one who said no and asked me to stay."

"You're always welcome here." Jack's expression softened. "I want you to consider this place your home, too."

Andy nodded, glad to know his brother felt that way. But this house *wasn't* his home, was it? It was his brother's home, and while Andy was more than happy to visit as often as possible, he didn't entirely belong here.

"So, to what do we owe the pleasure?" Jack asked as he moved around the kitchen, helping Blair.

They were synchronized, and the few times they weren't and bumped against each other, they always smiled and kissed. It was good to see, but it also hurt Andy a bit. Would he and Claude ever get to this point? For now, the distrust Claude seemed to have of guys made Andy feel like it would take a lot of work, and while he was up for that and not one bit afraid, he wished things were easier.

Although knowing what had happened between Blair and Jack before they got to this happiness made him feel better. Things would be hard until they weren't, and Andy would have to deal with whatever life threw at him.

"I wanted to ask Blair about Claude," he explained.

Jack turned, his eyes narrow. "I *knew* there was something

between the two of you. You spent the entire evening out on the porch with him yesterday."

Andy had settled at the counter. He looked down at his hands, wondering how much he should tell Blair and Jack. In the end, he decided to be honest. "I just wanted to see if he was okay. Our family can be a lot, and we were celebrating the adoption. Besides, he'd just learned about shifters."

"What happened between the two of you?"

"Nothing. We talked, and that's it." And he sucked in a breath. "But I found out he's my mate."

Something hit the floor, and Andy looked up to find out that Jack had dropped the box of spaghetti he'd taken out of the cupboard. Blair leaned down to pick it up while Jack swooped around the counter to drag Andy into a hug.

"Seriously? Claude is your mate?" he asked.

Andy nodded. "He is, but I didn't tell him."

"Why not?"

"Learning about shifters was a lot. He also told me about his ex and how he thinks relationships are trash." Those hadn't been his exact words, but it had been clear enough it was what he believed.

"I remember that asshole," Blair said with a growl.

Andy nodded at him. "I don't know if Claude told me everything, but even if he didn't, it was enough to make me hate that guy. I think that's one of the reasons I didn't tell him he's my mate. I could see he wouldn't take it well." Andy swallowed. "But Claude asked me to be his fake boyfriend at your work party at the end of the week."

Blair grinned. "And you agreed?"

"How could I have said no? I don't want to spook him and make him run, but I need to know more about him if I'm going to be there for him."

"I'll tell you everything I can," Blair promised. "But maybe you should take him out. Not on a date, but on a get-to-know-you dinner. He usually works late, so he'll still be at the office."

"I can do that, but first, tell me what you know." Andy settled in. He was relieved Blair would help him, although he wasn't sure it would change anything. Still, it was the first step for him to understand Claude better and hopefully convince him he was nothing like his ex-boyfriend.

Claude had forced himself to wait until lunchtime to text Andy. He'd been distracted all morning, and he'd hoped things would be better once he had, but instead, they were worse. He kept peeking at his phone, waiting for an answer that never came. Since he'd been a mess for most of the day, he'd decided to stay at work late, but his stomach was grumbling, which meant it was time to go home and have dinner.

Andy still hadn't answered.

Claude could see Andy had seen the message, and he wasn't sure what to think of it. Was Andy ghosting him? Claude wouldn't be surprised, but he didn't want to believe it. Andy hadn't seemed like a bad guy when they'd talked last night or last week. Besides, if Claude wanted to talk to him, it would be fairly easy to do so. He just had to visit Blair and wait, and eventually, Andy would pop out.

But Claude wasn't about to do that. He'd known asking Andy to be his fake boyfriend was a stupid idea the second the words had come out of his mouth. He'd been surprised Andy had said yes, but he wouldn't be if Andy changed his mind. Really, who would do something like this? It was ridiculous, and maybe it was a good thing that Andy seemed to have changed his mind.

Claude sighed and stared at his phone for a moment before shaking his head. He just needed to finish a few things. Then he'd head out, get something for dinner, and go home to mope. Hopefully, he'd get over the disappointment, and tomorrow morning, he'd be as good as new. He had to look forward, not backward. Who cared what Michael thought of him? He certainly didn't, and that wasn't why he'd asked Andy to be his fake boyfriend. No, he'd wanted to show Michael that he could find someone who treated him well, unlike Michael had.

But it didn't matter anyway. Michael might be pissed for a moment if he saw Claude with someone else, but he'd never loved him. He wouldn't think twice about him, and that was what Claude needed to do when it came to Michael.

His phone vibrated on his desk, and he snatched it up. His heart raced as he unlocked the screen, and a smile spread on his lips when he saw that Andy had finally answered.

But it wasn't the answer he'd expected.

Instead of telling him he'd be there at the party, Andy was asking him out.

I think we should have dinner together tonight.

Claude stared at the screen. His first instinct was to say *hell yes*, but he told himself to be cautious. *Tonight?* he texted back.

I know it's getting late, but I'm almost there.

He'd been so sure that Claude would say yes that he'd driven an entire hour to get to him? *What if I've already eaten?*

Andy sent a sad emoji. *Then you'll have to watch me eat or have dinner again. What do you think? Are you up at least for dessert?*

An image of Andy *being* dessert flashed in Claude's mind, but he pushed it away. Andy was nice, but Claude had told him he didn't want a relationship. He wasn't taking him out on a date. He probably just wanted to talk about the party or something like that. *I can eat dessert. I can eat dinner because I haven't yet.*

Great! Blair told me where the office is, so I'll be right there. I'm glad you said yes. I think this date will be perfect for getting to know each other and discussing the party.

Claude was relieved to read that Andy was still planning on coming with him. No matter what he'd told himself, he'd been afraid that wouldn't be true. *You know we can do that on the phone, right?* He texted.

I'd rather talk to you face to face.

Andy's words shouldn't make Claude's heart race, but they did. *I'll see you soon.*

I'll text you when I reach the office.

It didn't look like Andy would text anymore, so Claude put down his phone, got to his feet, and rushed to the bathroom. He used the facility, washed his hands and face, and tried to finger comb his hair so it didn't look like he'd been running his fingers through it most of the day like he had. He reminded himself that this wasn't a date and that he wasn't supposed to seduce Andy. Andy was here to talk and nothing else.

But Claude couldn't stop thinking that they could have talked on the phone and that Andy didn't have to drive an entire hour at this time of evening just to see Claude. It didn't make sense, and Claude didn't understand why Andy was doing it, but he told himself to believe what Andy had told him.

When Claude went back to his desk, it was to find Edgar leaning against it with his arms crossed over his chest. He arched a brow at Claude, and Claude suspected he could see how frantic he felt.

"Do you need anything else from me tonight?" he asked.

"Only for you to tell me what's going on. Also, I told you to go home a few times already. Why are you still here?"

"I was distracted, so I decided to stay a bit longer tonight." And it had been a good thing, what with Andy coming over to pick him up.

"Even distracted, you work more than half the people in this office. Now, tell me what had you behaving that way. And why are you bouncing on your feet?"

45

Claude wasn't sure he should tell Edgar about Andy. Edgar was family, though, halfway between a father figure and a best friend. Claude couldn't talk to his mother about any of this because she'd only tell him to run, but Edgar? He'd understand.

"I think I did something stupid," he said.

Edgar frowned. "What is it? You know you can tell me anything. I'll help you if I can."

This was what Claude needed, not his mother telling him to stay away from Andy. "You know last night when you reminded me about the party and that I needed to be there even though there's nothing I want less?"

"Look, if you don't want to be there, we can work something out. I believe you should face Michael, though."

Claude raised a hand. "I know. I'll be there. But that's where the stupid thing I did comes in. I asked Andy, one of Jack's brothers, to be my fake boyfriend for the duration of the party. He's about to pick me up so we can go to dinner and talk about that and everything else related to it." They'd have to come up with a story about how they met. Claude doubted Michael would ask, but just in case, he wanted to be ready.

Edgar's eyes had widened. "You really asked him that?"

"I did, and he said yes. I don't understand why, but I'm grateful. At least with him there, I won't have to face Michael alone. I know I should, but I'm not ready for that, and I don't know if I ever will be. I want him to disappear from my life and never see him again."

"I understand why you feel that way, and I hope things will get easier for you. As long as he's a client, though, we can't avoid him." Edgar pursed his lips. "But I'm tempted to dump him as a client."

"Don't. I don't need you to protect me that way, and I don't want the company to suffer because I chose the wrong guy. I'll be fine."

Edgar stared at Claude for a moment before nodding. "I think you will be. I can see why you're feeling awkward. You're out of your comfort zone, but I wouldn't say that what you did was stupid. A bit foolish, perhaps, and definitely impulsive, but as long as Andy's okay with it, why shouldn't you do it?"

"I'm terrified it's going to be a disaster."

Edgar laughed. "It certainly could become one, but I suggest you go with the flow. I don't know Andy well, but if he's anything like the rest of his family, he'll stand by your side and be there for you if you need him. He wouldn't have agreed to be your fake boyfriend otherwise."

"You're probably right." But Claude couldn't shake the feeling that something else was happening. Maybe it was the excitement at the thought of seeing Andy. Maybe it was knowing that no matter what happened at the party or tonight, there could never be anything between them.

Maybe it was the fact that for the first time since Michael, Claude wanted something to happen with a guy, even though he knew better.

Andy eyed the flowers on the passenger seat. He wasn't sure they were a good idea, but he hadn't wanted to pick up Claude empty-handed. He didn't want to freak Claude out and make him think this was a date, but that was how he felt.

Maybe this wasn't such a good idea, after all.

But it was too late to go back. Andy supposed he could throw away the flowers, but he didn't want to do that. He didn't have many details on Claude's relationship with his ex-boyfriend, but from what little he knew about the asshole, he suspected he hadn't been taking care of Claude. Claude was an adult and could take care of himself, but everyone enjoyed being cherished. Andy loved giving gifts, both at Christmas and birthdays or for no occasion at all. He hadn't wanted to go overboard, so he'd chosen flowers.

But he wanted Claude to feel important. He wanted him to see that he was nothing like Michael. Hopefully, this simple gesture wouldn't send Claude running. If it did, well, Andy would follow. He didn't care how long it took him to gain Claude's trust and to make him see he wasn't going anywhere. He'd do everything he could for that to happen.

He parked in front of the building, right behind a black car. It was clearly waiting for someone, too, so he texted Claude that he'd arrived. He wasn't sure how long he'd have to wait, but he didn't have anywhere better to be.

He looked around. He couldn't help but wonder how he and Claude would work things out if they ever got together. He wasn't as opposed to moving to the city as Jack had been, but it still wouldn't be his preferred option. He couldn't demand that Claude move to their little town, though. It wouldn't be right, especially not when Claude's job was so important to him. Andy could find work anywhere. Claude might be able to find something in their town, but it wouldn't be anything like what he did now. Besides, he'd have to stop working with Edgar, and Andy suspected that would be a hard no.

The door of the building opened, and Andy sat up straighter, but it wasn't Claude. Instead, Edgar strode out of the building toward the car in front of Andy. He turned slightly, and his eyes widened when he noticed Andy in the car.

Andy was surprised when Edgar leaned into the car to talk to the driver, then made his way toward him. He was suddenly nervous, and he wasn't even sure why. Edgar wasn't Claude's father. He was a good friend and a boss, but surely, he wouldn't tell Andy to stay away from Claude.

Andy swallowed and lowered his window as Edgar

reached it.

"Claude told me you were taking him out for dinner," Edgar said.

"I am. We're getting to know each other."

Edgar nodded. "He also told me you decided to help him with that fake relationship thing."

Andy hadn't expected Claude to tell Edgar about that. Edgar didn't seem angry, but Andy still found himself blurting out, "I won't hurt him the way Michael did. I wouldn't be able to even if I wanted to, and there's nothing I want less. He's my mate."

Edgar stared at Andy with wide eyes. "That was a lot of words in not a lot of time," he commented. "But I believe the most important ones were the last three."

Andy was behaving like an idiot. "Claude is my mate. I realized it last night, which is one of the reasons I said yes when he asked me to be his fake boyfriend."

Edgar nodded. "That's what I thought I'd heard." He frowned. "Let me tell you something about Claude."

"Isn't he coming down?"

"He is, but he likes to make sure I turned everything off in my office before doing so. He thinks I'd be entirely lost without him, and while that might be close to the truth, I *can* turn off my computer on my own."

And he liked that Claude cared, though. He took care of the people he loved, including Edgar.

Edgar leaned closer. "Claude and his mother have a complicated relationship. From what I saw the few times I met her, she's not a bad mother, but she's harsh, especially regarding relationships. She had two big failed ones, the first with Claude's father, the second with his sister's father. Neither of them is in the picture, and I don't believe Claude ever knew his father. His mother became bitter after her daughter's father left. I've met her a few times and heard a lot about her from Claude. She doesn't believe in relationships. She thinks that both she and her son are better off without men, and unfortunately, that has changed the way Claude views love. He tried with Michael, but you know how badly that went."

The situation was more complicated than Andy had expected. It didn't mean he'd give up, but he was worried.

Edgar smiled. "I'm not telling you this to discourage you. Since he's your mate, I know you'll be there for him and that you won't give up. I just want you to know what you're up against. It's not just Michael and the way his relationship with Claude ended. Claude's mother keeps whispering in his ear that he won't ever be happy in a relationship and that he should give up trying to find a good person to share his life with. She's poisoned his view of relationships, and it will be even harder for you after what happened with Michael. But I don't want you to give up. Claude deserves to be happy and wants someone in his life, no matter what his mother thinks. I hope that being his mate, you'll see that and that you won't abandon him."

"I promise I won't. I realize it'll be hard to crack Claude's shell, but I have all the time in the world to do so. Like you said, he's my mate, not just another guy."

"Good. And please, come to me if you have any problems. I'll do whatever I can to make sure Claude gives you a chance."

"Thank you." It was good to know that at least Edgar was on their side, since they clearly wouldn't have any kind of support from Claude's family.

That was fine. Andy had more than enough family for both of them, and he didn't care what Claude's mother thought.

The doors opened again, and there was Claude. He wore dress pants and a shirt under his jacket, and he was carrying his suit jacket and a tie in his hands, as well as a messenger bag. He'd opened the first few buttons of the shirt at the throat, and his hair shone under the light of the lamps.

He frowned when he saw Edgar talking to Andy and made his way toward them. "I thought you'd already went home," he told Edgar.

"I'm headed there now. I just recognized Andy and wanted to say hello."

"Is that all you said?"

Edgar laughed. "It is, don't worry." He stepped away from the car and closer to Claude. To Andy's surprise, he kissed the top of Claude's head. "Have fun tonight."

Claude flushed and looked away. "This isn't a date," he muttered.

Edgar winked at him. "Not yet. But it doesn't mean you can't have fun."

He strode toward the car still waiting for him, and Andy waited for Claude to climb into his car. He was even more nervous than before, but it was too late to take a step back. Besides, he didn't want to do that even if it hadn't been.

Whatever he had to face, whatever Claude believed about relationships, Andy was up for the challenge. He'd make Claude see that not everyone was like Michael or his mother's exes and that he could trust him with his heart.

Claude desperately wanted to know what Edgar and Andy had been talking about, but he knew better than to ask. In the end, it was none of his business, so he climbed into the car, or at least, he tried to. He saw just in time that there were flowers on the passenger seat, and he narrowly avoided sitting on them.

He picked up the bouquet, sat down, and closed the door. "Are these for me?" he asked.

It was a stupid question. He doubted Andy randomly went around with flowers in his car. He'd come here to talk to

Claude, which meant he'd brought the flowers for him.

"They are. I know this isn't a date, but I wanted to show you that not everyone is like Michael."

Claude wasted a few seconds putting on his seatbelt because he didn't know how to answer that. "I know that's not the case," he eventually said.

"But what happened with your ex-boyfriend still impacts you."

"That's because we haven't been broken up long."

"Want to talk about it some more?"

Claude shook his head. "The less I think about him, the better I feel. And thank you for the flowers. It was a thoughtful gesture." And one that already set Andy apart from Michael.

Claude raised the bouquet to his nose and took a deep breath. It was beautiful, and not the usual red roses he would have expected.

For one thing, it was bigger than Claude's head. There were a few orange roses, and Claude loved them, but that wasn't what caught his attention. He didn't know the name of most of the flowers, but he loved the big purple balls that shot out from the center of the bouquet. There was what might be freesia, also deep purple, and a lot of green leaves. There were flashes of light blue, dark and light pink, and orange. It smelled heavenly, and something in Claude's chest warmed.

Andy truly wasn't anything like Michael.

But he had to remind himself that they weren't together, no matter how nice Andy was. This wasn't a date, and he couldn't act like it was. Even if Andy was interested in him like that, Claude couldn't afford for his heart to be broken again. He was done with relationships, and he'd keep that promise he'd made to himself.

"I know it's a lot," Andy murmured.

"I love it." It would look good on Claude's coffee table, and he couldn't wait to wake up tomorrow morning and have breakfast while staring at it. "I don't think anyone has ever bought me flowers."

"That's a crime. Why wouldn't your ex-boyfriend buy you flowers?"

Claude shrugged. "I don't know. I guess most guys think it's a woman's thing."

"Do you think that?"

"No. I like flowers."

"Good." Andy appeared relieved. "I'll make sure to have flowers for you every time we meet."

Claude wanted to tell him it wasn't necessary, but the little thrill in his chest made him keep his mouth shut.

He stayed quiet until they reached their destination. Then his eyes widened, and he had to remind himself once again that this wasn't a date. It didn't matter that Andy had brought him flowers or that they both wore dress pants and a shirt. They were only here to talk about their fake relationship, and that was that.

"I hope you like French food," Andy said as he parked the car.

"You should probably have asked that earlier, but yes, I do. How did you get a reservation here?" The Swan was as classy and romantic as a restaurant could be. Claude had never eaten here, but from making reservations for Edgar, he knew that there was no way to get a table unless you were a regular, extremely rich, or reserved months in advance.

Andy's cheeks flushed. "I might have had help." He climbed out of the car, leaving Claude alone for a moment.

Edgar had been with Claude most of the day, so he wasn't the one who'd helped Andy. That only left Blair, and Claude would have words for him the next time they saw each other.

He set down the flowers as Andy opened his door. This felt more and more like a date, but Claude told himself that wasn't the case again.

"We can go elsewhere if you'd rather," Andy offered.

"No. This is perfect. I was just surprised."

Andy didn't look convinced, but he nodded and offered Claude his arm. Claude took it because why not?

They made their way to the restaurant. Andy looked uncomfortable as the maître d' guided them to a table at the back, but Claude was in his element. Even though he'd never eaten in this particular restaurant, he was used to this kind of place. Edgar liked good food and enjoyed having Claude with him during his lunch and dinner meetings.

Claude knew French cuisine, so he guided Andy through choosing his food. Once they'd placed their order and a waiter had brought them their drinks, Claude forced himself to relax.

This wasn't a date. It *wasn't*.

"So, how should we decide how we met and got together?" he asked, taking a sip of his wine.

"I think we should stay simple and as close to the truth as possible. We met during a family reunion. You were there because of Blair, and of course, I'm Jack's brother, so it makes sense. Maybe we started talking, spent most of the evening alone on the porch, and decided to give this a try."

"That would work, but I don't want Michael to think this is a recent thing."

"Then let's not mention Blair's birthday. We could've had a family reunion months ago."

"That sounds good." And it did, even though Claude felt ridiculous. He still didn't understand what he'd been thinking, but they were doing it.

He leaned over the table. "And we won't mention the shifter thing."

"I wouldn't dare. I don't know Michael or any of the people you and Edgar work with. It's better not to risk it."

Claude had expected it, so he wasn't surprised. "Do you

think you can answer a few questions about that?"

"Whatever you want to know."

Claude thought he had a good grip on what shifters were and what they could do, but he was curious about one thing. "Tell me about mates. Does it work like in romance novels?"

Andy leaned back in his chair. "Pretty much. I can't tell you how it actually works, but we know by scent. One sniff of our mate's scent, and we know."

"And do you bond, or something like that? That always happens in books."

Andy chuckled and shook his head. "No. We also don't live long lives or anything like that. We're like humans, except that we can turn into animals." His voice was softer now. "We're not superheroes. We want what every human wants, a home, love, a family, things like that. We don't always meet our mates, because what are the odds? But when we do, it's forever."

"It does sound like it would be hard to meet your mate if you only have one, but all of your brothers have, right?"

"They have. Everyone's stunned, and we don't understand how it could have happened, but in the end, it doesn't matter. They're happy and living their best life, and that's all we want for each other."

But Andy hadn't met his mate. "What about you?"

Andy hesitated, then shook his head. "My time will come eventually. I'm not in a hurry."

"I suppose you have time." Claude was twenty-eight, and he knew Andy was twenty-three. Andy could meet his mate tomorrow, next week, or in ten years. Claude was convinced that eventually, he would, but the thought didn't make him happy. If anything, it made him sad and angry because he wanted Andy for himself.

He forced a smile onto his face. No matter what he wanted, he knew what was best, and it wasn't to be with Andy. The fact that Andy could meet his mate at any second, even while dating someone like Claude, reinforced that knowledge.

There would be nothing between Claude and Andy, no matter how much Claude might want it.

CHAPTER FOUR

A ndy was nervous. He'd never been to such a posh party, and he hoped he wouldn't make a mess and embarrass Blair, Jack, and Claude. Knowing his luck, he'd spill one of the delicate champagne glasses all over someone's expensive evening gown or something.

The fact that he was super early didn't help. He'd been so nervous that he'd decided to head to the hotel where the party was being held. It was all glass and sharp angles, making Andy uncomfortable because it looked like none of the chairs and tiny couches where the guests were supposed to sit were comfortable. Only a few other people were already present, and he suspected they worked with Claude. He had no need to be early, but right now, he felt like a fool.

A waiter had noticed him, handed him a glass of champagne, and had promptly disappeared. Andy had parked himself in a corner, but he could see they were still setting things up, and he needed out of this situation.

He needed Claude.

But he had no doubt that Claude was busy, so instead, he took out his phone and texted his brother. Surely Jack would know what he should do. If Jack didn't, Andy might just hide on the patio he could see through the closed windows. It was windy and possibly too cold to hang outside, but it would be better than being here by himself and disturbing the waiters.

Help. I'm already here, and I'm the only one. What am I supposed to do?

Andy held his breath as he waited for his brother to

Catherine Lievens

answer. Jack was probably busy, so Andy wouldn't blame
him if he didn't, but he was relieved when the three dots
started dancing on his screen.

Doesn't the party start in half an hour?

Yeah.

Andy could imagine Jack laughing at him. He wasn't even
offended. He deserved to be laughed at, but he'd been so anxious to get here late that he'd arrived way too early. Surely,
he wasn't the only one who did things like that?

Come upstairs. Blair got us a room for the night.

Andy almost ran out of the room. He walked past the same
waiter who'd given him the glass of champagne earlier and
left his empty glass with him. Instead of making him more
relaxed, the alcohol made him want to puke, although that
could be more because he was nervous. Whatever the reason,
he didn't care. He just needed to hide until the party started.

He wanted to make a good impression but felt like a fool
instead. The clothes he was wearing didn't help. When Jack
had known he'd be at the party, he'd dragged Andy to get a
suit. Andy had protested because when would he wear this
kind of clothes again? But Jack had insisted, telling him that
Blair was paying and that Andy didn't need to worry about
anything. Andy didn't have anything to say against Blair paying—he was rich enough to buy him thousands of suits—but
it still felt odd to see Jack so comfortable with that. It meant
Jack was growing and that he and Blair were making things
work, and Andy wanted the same to happen between him
and Claude.

But he hadn't even told Claude they were mates yet.

He didn't know if he should. He wanted to, but tonight
wasn't the best time. Maybe Andy could think about it once
the party was over and Michael's ass had been kicked. The
party was important to Claude and his job, and Andy would
never do anything that could put that in jeopardy or distract
Claude.

58

But he didn't like it. Both he and his swan wanted Claude in their life, and it felt wrong to hide such an important fact from him. Claude had seemed in awe of the mate bond when they'd talked about it over dinner earlier in the week, and Andy hoped it meant that once he told him, Claude would accept it.

Andy had no way to know whether or not that would happen.

He understood why Claude was wary of men and relationships, and he couldn't imagine that seeing his ex-boyfriend at the party tonight would help with that. Maybe Andy should have told him they were mates sooner, and he almost had about a thousand times. Every time, though, he'd kept his mouth shut and had decided it wasn't the right moment.

But he was starting to wonder if the right moment even existed. He hadn't found it for now, and maybe he never would. Whatever happened next, though, he'd show Claude that he was here to stay and that he wasn't going anywhere. That was more than what Michael had been able to do, and it made Andy feel better to know that.

He headed upstairs, relaxing as he put more space between himself and the room where the party would be held. By the time he reached the room, he was even able to smile when Jack opened the door.

Jack looked Andy up and down. "You clean up well. Claude will be impressed."

Andy rolled his eyes and pushed past his brother. "I doubt he'll be able to focus on anything that isn't the party."

"I wouldn't be too sure about that," Blair said. He stood next to the window, working on his cufflinks. The top buttons of his shirt were still open, and he looked relaxed.

The way he smiled at Jack made Andy's heart ache, but he told himself that he and Claude would eventually have this. He just needed to give them time, and he had no problem doing so.

But waiting to tell Claude they were mates made Andy feel like he was doing something wrong. He had to remember that Claude was human, extremely busy, and dealing with his past relationship. It would be of no use to rush him into this.

Jack wasn't even wearing his shirt yet, but he strode toward Blair to help him with the cufflinks. Blair gave him a grateful smile, then turned his attention to Andy.

"He's been nervous for most of the week," he said.

Andy knew they were talking about Claude. "Because the party is important."

"It is, although I doubt it'll make or break any business deals. That's not why Claude was nervous. My father told me he had many questions about you and how to behave with you. I can't believe he asked you to be his fake boyfriend."

"I'll be the best fake boyfriend Claude could ever have."

"Maybe you could be his real boyfriend," Jack pointed out. "When will you tell him you're mates?"

Andy could see Jack was worried, and he didn't blame him. He was worried, too, but he'd decided not to rush Claude, and he'd do just that, no matter how anxious it made him. "Let him deal with the party first. I'll tell him he's my mate after that."

Jack looked at Andy for a moment before nodding. "As long as you remember that you need to tell him. He deserves to know."

"I'm aware of that. But we just met, and I want time to show him that we're meant to be together."

"I'm not sure that's going to work," Blair said as he reached for his tie on the desk by the window. "I wonder if knowing he's your mate will help. I mean, mates aren't just people who fall in love. We're destined to be together, and it's rare that a relationship between mates breaks up. Maybe that'll help Claude deal with his anxiousness when it comes to relationships."

Andy hoped so, but he wasn't ready to find out whether or not Blair was right. "After the party," he repeated.

Blair nodded. "Of course. This is your relationship, and you're the one to make decisions. Besides, I believe you're right and that it would be best to wait until the party is over. Just don't wait forever, all right? Claude won't be happy when he finds out you've hidden something this big from him."

Andy grinned. "As long as he gives me a chance, I don't care if he's angry at me."

Jack had disappeared into the bathroom, but he'd kept the door open. When he came back into the room, his shirt was on. "What shall we do to kill the time we have left before the party?"

Andy flopped into one of the armchairs in the sitting room area. "I don't know. Distract me, will you? I feel like I'm about to vibrate out of my skin."

Jack's smile was gentle. "I wouldn't worry too much if I were you. No matter what happened in Claude's past, he's your mate. It means something, and if you give him enough time, he'll accept it."

Andy could only hope his brother was right because he didn't know what he'd do if that wasn't the case.

Claude looked around the room, satisfied. He'd arrived twenty minutes before the party started, relieved to see that everything was on track. He'd been slightly late because he'd obsessed over what to wear. For some reason, he wanted to impress Andy, which meant he'd needed everything to be perfect, from his hair to the shine of his shoes. He doubted Andy would notice it, but it was important to Claude.

In the car on the way, he'd realized he hadn't thought

about Michael and what he'd think about the way he looked once.

Claude hoped that meant he was finally getting over his ex and the pain Michael had caused. Andy was a big part of that. They couldn't be anything more than friends, no matter how much he wanted them to be. He didn't understand why he felt that way, but he'd decided to push all those feelings aside until the party was over. He'd have time to obsess over Andy and how he made him feel later. For now, his entire focus should be on networking and ensuring everyone was happy.

An arm slid around his waist, startling him. He turned, ready to tell whoever it was to fuck off, only to find Andy smiling at him.

"You startled me," he said with a scowl.

Andy didn't look repentant. "You looked so good here, but also lonely."

Claude shook his head. "Not lonely. Busy."

"Makes sense. Everything's perfect, though."

He looked Claude up and down with a gaze that made Claude flush. What it would it be like to have Andy look at him the same way while they were both naked? He desperately wanted to find out, and it was getting harder to tell his heart he needed to resist. Andy was sneaking his way under Claude's skin and into his life, and Claude had no idea how to stop him.

The problem was that he didn't *want* to stop him.

No matter how many times he told himself he needed to keep his heart safe, that giving in would only hurt him, he could feel himself starting to cave. Andy was gentle, sweet, and just all-around nice. He was irresistible, and Claude didn't know how to deal with his feelings. He shouldn't have them, yet here he was.

A commotion by the door made him turn. Several guests had arrived earlier, but most of them were finally here. He started stepping away from Andy to be on hand in case anyone needed anything, then changed his mind and decided to stay where he was. He wasn't one of the event organizers. He was ready to help, but his job was done, and the only thing left for him to do was enjoy the party and be available if Edgar needed him.

He forced himself to relax. This wasn't the first work party he attended, and it wouldn't be the last. He knew how to do this, but Andy didn't, so he decided he'd stay by his side for most of the evening. He owed it to Andy, who was here to play his fake boyfriend just because Claude asked.

Claude moved until he could link his fingers with Andy's. "Hungry?" he asked.

Andy shook his head. "I'm too nervous to be hungry."

"You have nothing to be nervous about. Trust me. I've been to many of these parties, and you won't be the one to embarrass himself."

Andy laughed, getting the attention of a few people around them. Claude didn't care, though. He didn't care about anything but Andy and how nice he looked in his suit.

Waiters were circulating with platters heavy with glasses of champagne and tiny bits of food. Claude nibbled on several of them while talking to Andy, and he could tell that both of them were more relaxed now. It seemed that spending time together did them good, and he couldn't help but wonder what it meant. Was it possible that Andy felt the way Claude did? He had to be confused after Claude told him he was done with relationships, yet, he was here to help. He was a nice person that anyone would be lucky to have in their life, including Claude, no matter how many times he tried convincing himself that wasn't the case.

It was almost too easy to believe that he and Andy were actually together. Andy stuck close, parts of their bodies always touching. It was usually one of Andy's hands on

Claude's waist or their fingers brushing together. Andy's attention was all on Claude, making him feel like the most important person in the room.

And maybe to Andy, he was.

Claude had no idea what was happening, but he wouldn't solve this puzzle tonight.

Once they'd gone around the room once, he took Andy's hand and pulled him toward one of the tables by the wall. "Why don't we sit down for a bit?"

Andy looked relieved. "There are a lot of people."

"Shouldn't you be used to dealing with so many people? I mean, there are like fifty people in your family."

Andy laughed. The sound was warm and happy, and Claude felt smug that he'd been the one to cause Andy to feel that way. "We're not fifty," Andy said.

"It certainly felt like it both times I visited your family," Claude said as he sat down.

Andy sat next to him, and a waitress was with them only seconds later. Dinner wouldn't start until later, but Claude and Andy took a few more appetizers. This time, Claude got a glass of orange juice instead of champagne. He was too happy, and that could be dangerous in the situation. He didn't want to do something he and Andy would regret tomorrow morning.

Claude reclined back in his chair and looked around.

"Everyone is having fun," Andy said.

"It certainly looks like it."

"That's because they are. I know you weren't the one who organized this party, but you should be proud of your work."

Claude waved and his words away. "I was just a liaison between the various party organizers and the people in charge at the office. It was nothing."

"I'd have been lost if I'd had to do your job. If it was up to me, we'd be having this party in a fast food restaurant or something like that."

This time, it was Claude's turn to laugh. "I can imagine that all too well."

"There's no need to humiliate me," Andy said, smiling.

Claude had a hard time believing how well they fit together. He leaned closer, and it caused Andy's smile to widen. Claude couldn't remember the last time he'd felt so happy.

And then, everything came crashing down.

"Well, look who's here," a voice drawled.

Claude's back stiffened and he leaned away from Andy. He slowly turned, unsure if he was ready to face Michael. Either way, the moment had come.

Michael stood on the other side of the table, looking like a million bucks. He'd always looked great in a suit, and today wasn't any different. His black hair was perfectly combed, highlighting the square angles of his jaw. His nose was straight, and he looked like one of those Roman statues Claude had seen in museums.

And he wasn't alone.

Like Claude had expected, Michael had brought a twink with him. Claude wasn't sure it was the same guy he'd found in their bed, but he didn't care.

"I wasn't sure you'd be here," Michael continued. "Considering everything that happened." The guy with him leaned closer to him, quietly giggling. Claude resisted the urge to glare at the kid. He couldn't be more than twenty, if even that, and Claude was tempted to ask for his ID.

"Of course Claude had to be here," Andy said as he got to his feet. "This party wouldn't have happened if it weren't for him." He held out his hand and beamed. "I'm Andrew, Claude's boyfriend."

Michael stared at Andy's hand as if it might bite him. "Claude has a boyfriend?"

Andy didn't seem angry at the way Michael was snubbing

him. "I sure hope. I didn't catch your name."

Claude cleared his throat. "This is Michael. I've told you about him."

The smile never fell from Andy's lips, but from the way he looked Michael up and down, it was clear that whatever Claude had told him wasn't good. "I see."

There was no way Andy was doing it on purpose, but he was getting under Michael's skin, and he didn't even realize it.

Michael glared and straightened his back as if trying to show everyone around them who the tallest man was. "I have to say I'm surprised Claude told you about me."

"Oh, that was when we talked about our disastrous previous relationships," Andy said smoothly. "Why don't the two of you sit with us?"

Claude was horrified at Andy's suggestion, but he wasn't about to make a scene. Still, he'd make sure to strangle Andy as soon as he was alone with him.

The traitor.

Andy hoped Michael would say no. He didn't like the guy, but maybe it was because he was firmly on Claude's side. He was biased, and while he wasn't about to become Michael's best friend, he didn't want Claude to be embarrassed or to have to deal with Michael's foul mood.

But Michael and his date didn't sit down. Instead, he stared at Andy as if he'd asked him to spread his date out on the table and sacrifice him to the gods.

He didn't even answer. He dismissed Andy with barely a glance and turned his attention back to Claude.

"So, I hear you're still a personal assistant," he said.

His voice told Andy what he thought of that. He tightened his hands into fists, but since he couldn't hit the asshole, he sat back down and wrapped an arm around Claude's shoulders.

"I am," Claude said tightly.

"And he does such a good job." Andy beamed. "Edgar is over the moon happy with Claude's job. He keeps trying to convince him to take a promotion, but Claude won't. He cares too much about what he does."

Claude looked at Andy as if he wasn't sure whether he wanted to strangle or kiss him. Andy hoped he'd choose the second option.

"You call Mr. Syme by his first name?" Michael asked, sounding stunned.

Andy grinned at him. "Of course. He's family, after all. Why wouldn't I call him by his first name?"

Michael's eyes narrowed. "How did you say the two of you met?"

Andy relaxed. "At a family meal. My brother was eager to introduce us to his new partner, and Blair's parents, along with Claude, were there. I was there because Blair's boyfriend is my brother."

Michael blinked. "You're Blair's brother-in-law?"

"Oh, you know Blair?"

"Not in person." And Michael sounded pissed by that.

"Such a pity. I'd put in a good word, but considering you and Claude were together and that it didn't end well, it's probably best if I don't." He got to his feet again and offered Claude his hand. "Now, why don't we go out there and mingle for a while? I'm sure you have dozens of people to introduce me to."

Claude appeared relieved that Andy was giving him an out. He quickly stood up and took Andy's hand. "You're right. Everyone wanted to meet you once they found out you'd be at the party, so we should probably start." He turned back to Michael. "I'd say it was a pleasure seeing you, but it wasn't. I hope never to see you again."

Michael stared, his jaw slack, while Andy allowed Claude to drag him away, trying hard not to laugh.

As soon as they were far away from Michael, he chuckled. "Did you see his face?"

"I never want to see his face again," Claude grumbled. "And what was that?"

"What was what?"

"The whole everyone *loves him and is so happy with his work thing*. What was that about?"

Andy shrugged. "Just the truth."

"How would you know?"

"I might not know many people in the company, but I do know Blair and Edgar, and they're happy with your work."

"That's because they consider me family."

Andy shook his head. "It's because you're good at what you do. I can see Michael did a number on you and that maybe, you lost some trust in yourself. I wish you could see yourself the way I see you." To Andy, Claude was the world. He was the best person Andy could have chosen as his mate, and he couldn't wait for them to start their life together. Hopefully, now that the Michael thing was out of the way, they'd be able to do just that.

Claude stared. "You believe all the things you said?"

Andy looked around. He wanted to drag Claude away and give him a moment to relax, but he doubted they'd be able to manage it in this room. It was full of people talking, laughing, and not at all private.

He took Claude's hand again, looked around one last time, and pulled him through the nearest door. As soon as it closed behind them, silence blanketed them. They were in a hallway, so it would be easy for anyone to interrupt them, but everyone was so busy with the party that Andy doubted that would happen.

"I believe every word I said," Andy told Claude, crowding

him against the wall.

Claude's eyes were wide, but he didn't protest. He swallowed heavily and continued staring at Andy.

"I know there are many things you didn't tell me about yourself, including details about your relationship with Michael," Andy continued. "And I understand. You and I barely know each other, and what happened with your ex-boyfriend is none of my business. But please, believe me when I tell you that you're one of the nicest men I know."

Claude made a strangled sound. "Maybe you don't know many nice people, but I assure you they exist."

"I know. I have one of them in front of me."

Claude shook his head. "I don't know what I've done to earn all of this from you, but I'm grateful. I still believe you don't see me how you should."

Andy was done with all of this. It was clear that Claude wouldn't believe anything he said, and Andy didn't know how to convince him to see the truth in front of him. No matter what Michael said or thought, Claude was perfect, or at the very least, perfect for Andy. In the end, that was all that mattered.

Andy leaned closer. Claude's eyes had already been wide, but they got even wider, something Andy hadn't thought was possible. He stared at Andy as Andy pressed against him, but he didn't push him away. And he hoped it was a good thing and decided to take a risk.

He cupped the back of Claude's head and pulled him close. Their lips met, and Andy sighed in pleasure and relief.

Finally.

That was the only thing Andy could think. He'd wanted to kiss Claude since the first time he'd seen him, and he could hardly believe he finally was. He wanted so much more, but he had to be conscious of where they were and what was happening around them. It wouldn't do anyone any good to make a public display of their affection beyond a few kisses and holding hands.

So, Andy reined himself in. The party had to be a success for Claude and everyone else who worked with him, and Andy wouldn't be the one to embarrass them and ruin everything. Still, he couldn't stop kissing Claude, and he kept on brushing their lips together, enjoying the tiny sounds of pleasure coming from Claude.

"You kissed me," Claude said when Andy finally forced himself to lean back.

Andy looked down at him. His cheeks were flushed, and he'd never looked better. Andy was tempted to drag him to the hotel lobby, get a room, and keep him there the entire night, but now wasn't the best moment to do that. Hopefully, later, it would happen.

"You let me kiss you," he said.

Claude's cheeks flushed a deeper red. "What was I supposed to do?"

Andy frowned because that wasn't the answer he'd wanted. "If you didn't want me to kiss you, you should have pushed me away."

Claude hesitated, then shook his head. "I did want you to kiss me."

"Are you sure? Because if you didn't, please, let me know. I won't do it again."

"But what if I want you to do it again?" Claude asked in a whisper.

"Then I will."

Claude needed more, but they couldn't do anything in a hallway right next to where the party was still in full swing. Claude typically wouldn't have left until it was over and everyone had gone home, but right now, he couldn't have cared less about any of that. He wanted Andy to kiss him again and to do so much more, but where could they go? Claude's apartment was way too far.

Andy leaned down and kissed Claude again. Claude groaned and let Andy press him against the wall. He forgot where they were and why this was a bad idea until a door close by opened. The noise of the party became louder, then softer again as the door closed, but it was enough to jolt Claude into action.

They were in a hotel. That meant they could get a room, right?

He grabbed Andy's hand and pulled him along. Andy laughed but followed, stumbling on the carpet before getting his feet under him.

"Where are you taking me?" he asked.

He sounded breathless, and Claude needed more of that. "To get a room."

"Oh? And what are you planning on doing in that room?"

Claude turned to glare. "What do you think?"

Thankfully, Andy didn't ask if Claude was sure. Claude had no idea of what he'd have done if Andy had, but he'd turn around and go back if he allowed himself to think too much about this. He and Andy weren't together, and they weren't planning on changing that. They probably shouldn't be having sex, but Claude didn't care about what they should or shouldn't do.

Andy grinned. "In that case, I could take you to my room."

Claude frowned. "You have a room here?"

"Yep. So do Jack and Blair. They decided it would be better so they could both drink, and since I didn't want to drive home after the party, I did the same."

"Why didn't you say so sooner? Let's go."

Andy laughed again, then took the lead.

Claude let him because he had no idea where they were going. He didn't care much, either. He just needed a bed and to get Andy naked.

All hotels were similar—long hallways that felt like a maze, soft music in the elevator, carpet that softened the sound of footsteps. They stopped on the third floor, where Andy went to the right. They walked, passing several doors until Andy stopped in front of one and took out a keycard from his pants pocket.

Claude waited until the door was open. Then he pushed Andy inside, both of them stumbling as Claude reached back and slammed the door shut. The sound was loud, but he ignored it, grabbed Andy's tie, and pulled him close to kiss him again. He felt as Andy fumbled for something on the wall, and seconds later, light flooded the room.

"What are you doing?" Claude asked.

"I want to see you."

"You'll be too busy to look at me." Claude turned, already working on his tie, and froze. "Why is there a bottle of lube on your bed?" he asked.

Andy groaned. "Jack. Dammit. I'm going to kill him."

Claude wasn't sure how to feel about Andy's brother knowing what he and Andy would be doing.

"Should I tell him he ruined the mood next time I see him?" Andy asked.

Claude resumed his work on his clothes. He threw his tie in the direction of the desk, then shrugged out of his jacket and unbuttoned his shirt. The next thing to go was his undershirt, but then Andy caught Claude's hand.

He pulled at it so quickly that Claude had no other choice than to go. He looked up at Andy to see him smile. It made his heart beat faster. In the short time he'd known Andy, he'd never seen him smile like that. It was happy but also wishful, which made him want to ask Andy questions that were better left unsaid.

The temperature in the room rose as Andy cupped

Claude's cheek with his free hand. Claude waited for Andy to kiss him, but instead, he just stared for a moment. Claude wished he hadn't. He felt like Andy could see right through him, which made him feel exposed and vulnerable, something he'd promised himself he'd never let happen again.

Claude reached up and grabbed Andy's wrist.

"Are you sure about this?" Andy asked.

Claude kissed him without answering. He wasn't sure of anything except that he wanted skin, and he wanted it now. Thankfully, Andy seemed to be on board with that, because he kissed Claude back.

Claude moaned, his mouth opening to welcome Andy. Andy's tongue slipped in, taking possession of it and of Claude's entire being. Claude lost himself in the kiss, but he felt it when Andy guided him backward. The back of his knees bumped against the mattress, and he folded back, eager for whatever Andy would give him.

Andy went down with him, landing on top of Claude. Claude didn't mind the extra weight — far from it.

They continued kissing. Claude was more than happy to ignore the need to breathe, but he couldn't do so forever. Panting, he wrenched his mouth away from Andy's and stared at the ceiling as Andy licked down Claude's jaw. He paused at his neck as if he knew that any kind of attention there made Claude's knees go weak.

Maybe he did. He had an uncanny ability to read Claude.

"You're still wearing pants," Andy grumbled.

His hands moved down to hook under Claude's belt.

"And you're still wearing everything," Claude answered. "Including your jacket."

Andy placed one of his elbows next to Claude's face and looked at him. Andy was beautiful, and Claude couldn't believe this was happening. At that moment, he wanted Andy for eternity, and he allowed himself to believe that maybe he'd have him.

Andy still had a hand on Claude's belt. He fumbled with it, and Claude reached down to help, but he felt it slacken before he could. Andy's lips descended on Claude's again, the kiss hungry and hot and enough to distract Claude. Fingers skimmed his belly button, then one of his nipples.

"You're still overdressed," he mumbled.

He couldn't wait to get his hands on Andy's skin and touch as much of it as possible. He jerked Andy's shirt out of his pants, then pushed it up, uncaring if he ruined it. He ran his palms up and down Andy's back, feeling smooth muscles move under his touch.

Claude's nails dug in when Andy's mouth latched on his right nipple. He was probably leaving marks. The thought thrilled him. He wanted Andy to remember this moment, and the slight pain would make sure he did. Andy seemed to want to mark him, too, because he closed his teeth around the nipple he'd been teasing and bit down. He released when Claude bowed his back and blew cool breath on his moist, tender skin.

Andy grinned. With his flushed cheeks and wide eyes, he looked debauched, yet he still hadn't lost his jacket.

Andy kissed his way down Claude's abdomen, taking his time, learning his way around Claude's body as he finally undid Claude's pants and slowly slid them down his legs along with his underwear, leaving kisses every few inches.

He made Claude feel cherished and loved, which was all Claude had ever wanted. For one night, he wanted to allow himself to believe that all of this was true and that he'd have this tomorrow, next week, next *year*—forever. He'd have to come back to reality soon enough. He could give himself an hour to believe his dreams had come true.

Andy paused to remove Claude's shoes and socks, and when he finally had Claude naked, he stood and looked at him. Claude didn't hate his body, but he also didn't love it. He knew he could be slimmer and have more muscles, but he'd never cared much about any of that. He still couldn't help but wonder if Andy liked what he saw.

"You're the most beautiful man I've ever seen," Andy murmured reverently.

Claude's entire body flushed. He wasn't sure he believed it, but it was one more thing he decided to go along with for the night.

He couldn't allow Andy to see how his words touched him. "Well, I'm naked, but you're not, and I'd like to see what I'm working with." It would be incredibly sexy to have Andy fuck him fully dressed, but Claude would only have tonight, and he wanted Andy naked.

A slow grin spread on Andy's face. He was quick as he shed his jacket and tie and unbuttoned his shirt. Everything landed somewhere on the carpet, and Claude's mouth went dry as Andy's masculine body was slowly revealed.

Andy's skin glowed in the soft light, and while Claude wanted to touch, he told himself to wait and watch. He took in Andy's strong shoulders and the way the muscles of his stomach bunched as he took off his undershirt. A smattering of dark hair covered Andy's chest, thinning to a trail that ended at his belly button. He didn't have a six-pack, but his stomach was flat.

When he pushed down his pants, Claude couldn't resist anymore. Raising on all fours, he pressed a hand to Andy's chest, marveling at the sensation when it moved. His body responded, his cock jerking and yearning.

Andy dropped the last of his clothing and grabbed Claude's shoulder. He gently pushed until Claude got the hint and spread out on his back, opening his legs and exposing himself. It had been a while since the last time he'd been fucked, and even though he'd never admit it, he was grateful for Jack's gift.

Andy settled between Claude's legs and opened the lube.

Suddenly Claude was nervous. Was he doing the right thing? He and Andy weren't together, but he'd seen how Andy looked at him. He didn't want to give Andy false hope, but he also wanted to lose himself in this for a moment. It would be over too soon, leaving only memories that Claude would cling to if the loneliness ever became too bad.

"You're thinking too much," Andy murmured. "We'll do whatever you're ready for. Just tell me."

How could he be so perfect? Why couldn't Claude have him? He supposed he could, and he did, but not for long. It would break his heart if he fully opened it to Andy and Andy decided he'd had enough a few months from now.

All coherent thoughts fled Claude's mind when he felt a slick finger prodding at his hole, gently circling it. "I thought you wanted me to tell you what I was ready for?" he asked, his voice sounding like it belonged to someone else.

"You weren't telling me, so I decided to experiment."

Andy leaned down and licked Claude's cock. Claude moaned and thrusted up, hoping Andy got the message that he very much wanted this. He must have, because he proceeded to make Claude crazy with lust, using his hands, tongue and lips—and teeth.

It was almost too much. Claude was barely aware that Andy was stretching him until one of his fingers brushed against his prostate, because he was so focused on Andy's mouth on his cock. The pleasure threatened to pull Claude over the line, but it was too soon. He wanted Andy inside him.

"Come up here," Claude commanded. "I need you."

Andy moved quickly, lifting Claude's legs and positioning himself between them after cleaning his fingers on the white sheet . Claude was relieved to see him roll a condom on his cock without him having to ask. After what had happened with Michael, he'd been cautious.

Andy didn't hesitate as he slowly pushed in, making Claude whimper. He was as eager as Claude and wanted him as much as Claude did.

This was all Claude had ever wanted. Andy fucked him slowly, pushing and pulling until he was completely seated, then pausing. Claude pulled him down to kiss him because he couldn't bear to look him in the eyes. He felt too raw, especially knowing this was a one-time experience.

He wasn't sure Andy understood that, and the moment wasn't right to tell him.

Claude wrapped his legs around Andy's waist, locking them in place. His cock rubbed against Andy's stomach as Andy fucked him. He pushed a hand between them and wrapped his fingers around his cock, jacking himself off awkwardly. Andy sat up, taking Claude with him. His hands were on Claude's hips, helping him maintain the rhythm.

"Andy," Claude groaned.

Andy tilted his hips, and the next time he slammed in, he hit Claude's prostate. Claude cried out, briefly wondering if the people in the neighboring rooms had heard him and not caring if they did.

Andy's grin was feral as he continued thrusting until Claude felt like he was about to explode. He pulled on his cock one last time. Then his entire body contracted as he came.

Andy rocked them through their orgasms. Right now, he was a part of Claude, but the dream was almost over.

Claude screwed his eyes shut. He wanted to cry, and it was so fucking tempting to stay the night and wake up in Andy's arms.

But he couldn't. Opening his heart would mean that Andy could break it, and Claude couldn't go through that again.

They couldn't stay like this forever, unfortunately.

Andy gently lifted Claude off his lap, spreading him out on

the comforter so he could get up. He dealt with the condom, then disappeared into the bathroom and came out with a wet towel.

Claude looked away as Andy cleaned him. The tenderness of the gesture made him want to scream. Why couldn't he have this? Why couldn't he be happy with Andy? Why couldn't Andy be his forever?

Andy climbed back into bed and drew Claude against his chest. He sighed deeply and kissed Claude's forehead.

Claude settled in. He had to leave, but he didn't want to hurt Andy more than he was already about to by getting up and going now. He supposed Andy would still be hurt and confused when he didn't find him here tomorrow morning, but he had to go. He couldn't stand saying goodbye and explaining that they were over before they'd even started because he was terrified Andy would break his heart.

So, once he was sure Andy was asleep, Claude slipped out of bed, grabbed his clothes, threw them on, and left.

CHAPTER FIVE

Andy was alone when he woke up. For a few moments, he thought that maybe Claude was in the bathroom, but he couldn't hear anything, and the bathroom light was off. With dread clutching at his gut, he got out of bed and looked around the room.

There were no traces of Claude. His cell phone and suit were all gone. It was as if he'd never been there, and it hurt to see that. It hurt even more to realize that Claude had run away. Why had he left? Had something gone wrong last night? Andy couldn't remember anything that would have sent Claude running, but maybe he was wrong. Maybe he'd done something that Claude hadn't wanted, and instead of speaking up, he'd waited until Andy was asleep to run.

Andy had a choice. He could either go home with his tail between his leg, knowing Claude would stay away from him, or he could do something about it. Would it be wrong for him to go find Claude? If Claude had wanted to talk to him, he could have, but instead, he'd left. What did that say about what Claude wanted?

Maybe if Claude had been just another guy, Andy would have gone home to lick his wounds. But Claude wasn't just a guy. He was Andy's mate, and Andy wasn't going to lose him without a fight. If Claude didn't want to be with him, he'd deal with it. It would break his heart, but he wouldn't have a choice. He wanted to know why Claude had fled, though. Was it because of Andy and something he'd done or was he afraid?

Claude had been honest about the fact that he didn't think he'd ever have a relationship again after Michael. Edgar had warned Andy that considering how Claude's mother was and what she thought of relationships, it wouldn't be a surprise if Claude did everything he could to keep Andy away. Was that what was happening? Had he run before Andy could hurt him?

Andy rubbed his face. He wanted to believe that was the truth, because that was hopefully something he could fix. If Claude didn't like him and this was only sex for him, Andy wouldn't be able to do anything about it. If Claude wanted something more with Andy but needed reassurance that Andy wasn't going anywhere, then, hopefully, Andy could do that.

He got out of bed and stretched. He suspected he knew where Claude had gone, but he needed to be sure. The only way to do that was to find Blair or Edgar, and since Blair was in the same hotel, he was easily accessible.

Andy showered, put on his dress pants and shirt, and carried his suit jacket and his tie out of the room. He made his way toward the room Blair and Jack shared, hoping they'd know where Claude was.

When he knocked, it took them a moment to answer. Jack was the one who did, and he glared at Andy when he saw him. "What are you doing here? Where did you disappear to last night? I looked for you."

Andy couldn't help but feel smug about the night he and Claude had spent together. "I was with my mate."

Jack's eyes widened. "You were? What happened? Where is he?"

"Can I come in?"

Jack's eyes narrowed, but he nodded and stepped to the side.

He was wearing a pair of sweatpants, while Blair was

already fully dressed. He peeked out of the bathroom when he heard Andy come in, but his smile turned to a frown. "I thought you said you'd spent the night with Claude?" he asked as he walked into the room.

"I did. He ran away during the night."

Jack made a strangled sound. "He did *what?*"

Andy was already tired, and it was barely nine AM. "You heard me. We spent the night together, but when I woke up, he wasn't there."

"Did you tell him he's your mate?"

"I didn't have the opportunity."

Jack groaned. "Of course you didn't tell him."

"Do I have to remind you that you ran away from Blair not so long ago?"

Jack's glare was epic. "We're not talking about me. We're talking about you. You do realize that telling Claude he's your mate would probably have solved all your problems before they even started?"

"I don't know about that. The only thing I do know is that he left, and I need to find him." Andy looked at Blair. "Where would he be on a Sunday morning?"

"Normally, I'd say home, but considering what you just told us, I wouldn't be surprised if he's gone to work. He usually waits until Monday after parties to look into how everything went and make sure everything gets cleaned up, but if he's trying to forget what happened between the two of you, he'll try to distract himself with work."

"So I'll find him at the office?"

Blair nodded. "Probably. I'll contact the guard downstairs and tell him to let you pass."

"You'd do that for me?"

"If you were anyone else, I wouldn't, but you need to talk to Claude. I can see you're falling for him, and I suspect he feels the same but that he's letting his fears dictate his

81

behavior. Try to make him see that he can have a relationship and be happy with you. That's all we want for him."

That was all Andy wanted, too, and he had a chance to make it happen. He just hoped Claude would listen to him, mostly because he didn't know what he'd do if his mate didn't. Could he go back to a life without Claude in it? Would he ever be able to forget Claude and throw himself into a new relationship?

Now wasn't the moment to think about that. Andy couldn't go there thinking that Claude would reject him. He had an ace up his sleeve, and since Claude knew about mates and what they meant, hopefully he'd see that Andy was the one guy who'd never leave him behind.

Andy headed out, dreading what was about to happen. He needed it to go well, and while he realized that having Claude accept him wouldn't solve all their problems, it would be the first step to being in a real relationship. He enjoyed playing fake boyfriend, but he wanted and deserved so much more, and so did Claude. Hopefully, Claude would see that and agree with Andy.

Andy drove to the building where Claude worked, parking in the almost empty parking lot. The only other car there was Claude's, and Andy was relieved to see that Blair was right.

The guard at the entrance stopped him, but only until Andy told him his name. Once he had it, he waved him to go upstairs, and Andy stepped into the elevator. He tapped his foot along with the rhythm of the music, needing an outlet for his anxiety.

He was about to talk to Claude, and he had no idea how things would go. If Claude had been anyone else, Andy would be positive they could work things out and be together. With Claude, he wasn't sure of anything, and it made him want to run instead of making himself vulnerable.

But no matter whether or not he talked to Claude, he was

still in too deep. It would hurt, either if he left without talking to his mate or if his mate rejected him.

The elevator stopped. Andy's heart was in his stomach. He swallowed and stepped out, looking around to orient himself. Blair had told him where Claude worked, so it was easy to find his desk — and him.

Claude was busy, his head bent over his cell phone. For a moment, he didn't look up, focused on what he was doing. Then Andy cleared his throat to get his attention, and his head snapped up. His eyes widened, and he stared as Andy stared back.

Claude had been thinking about Andy. How could he not? He'd spent the best night of his life with a guy, and he'd run away before they could talk about it. He'd suspected Andy wouldn't take that lying down, and he was right. He just hadn't expected Andy to hunt him down at work, especially on a Sunday.

Claude had believed Andy would go home, maybe try calling or texting. In the end, there wasn't anything between them. They'd been fake boyfriends for the time of the party, had gone out once, and had texted several times. That didn't make a relationship, especially when Claude didn't want one and couldn't afford to have one.

Yet Andy was standing in front of him.

Claude got to his feet. "What are you doing here?"

Andy crossed his arms over his chest. Claude couldn't tell if he was angry or just annoyed. He also wasn't sure why Andy was here, and he didn't want to let himself hope it was because Andy cared about him.

Maybe Andy did. They were connected through their families, and maybe that was why Andy was here. He wanted to make sure Claude was okay and that what had happened between them wouldn't mess up anything.

But it had already messed something up. Claude's heart was in shambles, and he had no idea how to deal with it.

"What do you think I'm doing here?" Andy asked instead of answering.

"I wouldn't have asked if I knew."

Andy sighed, and his shoulders slumped.

Claude didn't know him all that well, but he didn't like seeing how defeated he looked. He especially disliked knowing it was because of him, but what could he do? He couldn't afford to have a relationship. That much, he was sure of. He'd have to let Andy down nicely, but was there any way to make that happen?

"You ran," Andy said.

Claude shook his head. "I came to work."

"And I have no doubt that you're here because you thought I wouldn't find you."

Claude looked away. He wasn't about to admit it, but it was correct. "Well, I have things to do."

"That's not true," Edgar said as he walked in.

Claude glared at him, his attention temporarily on his boss. "And what are *you* doing here? Mathilde will be pissed when she finds out you came into work on a Sunday."

"She knows I'm here and that it's because you're being an idiot. We both want you to realize that and to make sure you're okay."

Claude narrowed his eyes. "I'm being an idiot?"

Edgar gestured at Andy as if Claude had needed that to know what he was talking about.

He was horrified. "How do you know what happened between Andy and me last night? Were you spying on us?" Claude looked at Andy. "Or did you tell him we spent the night together?"

Edgar made a strangled sound. "You spent the night

together?"

Claude realized that his boss hadn't known where he'd spent the night. His cheeks flushed, and he wished the floor would open beneath his feet and swallow him whole. Unfortunately, that didn't happen, and he found himself the center of both Edgar's and Andy's attention.

"Well, that's good news," Edgar finally said.

"It would be good news if he hadn't left while I was sleeping without telling me anything," Andy grumbled.

"You did that?" Edgar asked Claude.

Claude glared at him. "Correct me if I'm wrong, but you're my boss, and you have no business sticking your nose in my personal life."

"I might be your boss, but that's not all I am." Edgar raised his hands as Claude's glare deepened. "But I get what you're saying. You're right, and I have no place telling you what to do or not do." He hesitated. "But, please, give Andy time to explain. I know Michael hurt you and that your mother has been telling you that relationships aren't worth it since you were a child, but this is something you have to decide on your own. You can't allow anyone to ruin your relationship with Andy. It's important."

Claude had no clue what was happening or why Edgar was saying this. "I don't understand."

Edgar shook his head. "Go with Andy. Allow him to explain, and please, for the love of everyone you care about, give him a chance. Don't shield your heart just because you think it's what you should do. You can't spend the rest of your life alone, Claude. You're only twenty-eight."

Claude couldn't deny he'd thought that being on his own for the rest of his life would be lonely, but he wasn't sure he could open up enough to the possibility of pain to get in another relationship.

He looked at Andy. He supposed he'd find out soon

enough. He wasn't sure what Andy wanted to tell him, but part of him wanted Andy to admit he was in love with him. It was stupid, but in the end, the thing Claude wanted the most was to be loved.

Andy might just be the right person to do that. He *would* be the right person if Claude wasn't terrified of getting hurt.

Claude sighed. "Fine. I'll listen to what Andy has to say. But you have to go home, Edgar."

"I'll go once I'm done here. Call me if you need anything later, even if it's only to talk."

Claude didn't see why he should call Edgar, but he nodded anyway because otherwise Edgar wouldn't leave him alone.

He and Andy waited until Edgar's footsteps had faded and he was in his office. When Andy didn't say anything, Claude decided he might as well get it over with. "Why don't we head to the roof?"

"What's on the roof?" Andy asked.

"A few chairs and a table. It's not much, but it helps when the office becomes too much. It can be crowded during the week."

Andy looked around. "It's not crowded right now."

"I need some fresh air." And Claude didn't want to come back to work tomorrow and have to sit by the place where Andy told him he never wanted to see him again—or where he told him he loved him.

Claude had no idea which one he wanted to happen the most.

That was a lie. He knew which way he wanted this to go. That didn't mean it would happen, and not just because of Andy. Claude suspected that *he* was the biggest problem between the two of them, and the fear felt like a living thing deep in his chest and stomach. It clutched at him, trying to pull him back, telling him that he couldn't have this. It was way too easy to think of how much Andy could hurt him, even though Claude didn't want to believe it would happen.

Andy followed Claude to the elevator, and they headed up. The office was empty, which was a relief.

It was windy outside, but Claude didn't care. The few chairs he'd brought up here along with the table were tucked close to the wall, which helped. He huddled in one of them, waiting for Andy to say whatever he'd come here to say. He wanted the disappointment and fear to be over quickly, and maybe once it was done, he could go home and mope over what had happened. Hopefully, by the time he saw Andy at the next family dinner, lunch, or whatever, he'd be over the heartbreak that was mostly his fault.

"Why did you leave?" Andy asked quietly.

"Well, I didn't know if you'd want me to be there when you woke up." That was the easiest way to answer, even though it wasn't entirely the truth.

"Why wouldn't I want you to be? I wouldn't have spent the night with you if I didn't like you and didn't want more of it. I'm not a one-night stand kind of guy. Besides, I thought you liked me."

Claude swallowed. "I do." Much more than he should. Much more than was safe for his heart. "But I didn't want to make things awkward. Our relationship was fake."

Andy snorted. "The relationship might have been, but the sex wasn't."

Claude wasn't embarrassed by what they'd done. He wanted it to happen again. He just wasn't sure it would.

"Look, you agreed to be my fake boyfriend for the party, and you did just that. What happened after the party, well, we can forget about it. It doesn't have to mean anything. Your life isn't here, and besides, I don't do relationships anymore. I thought it would be easier to leave you while you were asleep. That way, things wouldn't have turned awkward."

Andy was silent for a moment, and Claude had to look at

him. When he did, it was to find Andy frowning.

"You don't think we can make this work?" Andy asked.

"I don't think there's anything to make it work." Claude's heart broke, but he needed to say the words. He needed to convince at least himself of what he was saying.

Andy shook his head. "That's not true."

"You can't tell me you want a relationship with me. I told you I was done with that."

"You might be, but I'm not, and you're my mate. Would you take that away from me?"

Claude's brain was stuck on the words. He couldn't make sense of them, no matter how hard he tried.

He was Andy's mate?

Andy held his breath as he waited. This probably wasn't the best way to tell Claude he was his mate, but he didn't know how else to do it. Claude either couldn't see what was right in front of him, or he didn't want to see it. He was so stuck in his belief that he shouldn't have relationships that he wasn't allowing himself to see that Andy cared about him and that he wouldn't leave him.

Andy hoped that telling him he was his mate would help Claude realize that he wasn't going anywhere and would allow him to relax and give him a chance, but he wasn't entirely sure, and it made him anxious.

"I'm your mate?" Claude asked.

"You are," Andy confirmed.

"You're sure about that? There's no mistake?"

Andy shook his head. "There can't be a mistake. I knew when I sat on my parents' porch next to you. I smelled you, and my world changed."

Claude got to his feet. He started pacing in front of Andy, and Andy couldn't tell if it was a good or bad thing. What he *could* tell was that Claude was full of nervous energy that he needed to deal with. If pacing was his thing, Andy didn't have a problem with it.

"I'm your mate, and you've known for a week, yet you didn't tell me."

This was one of the things Andy had been afraid of. "I should have," he said. "I regret not doing so sooner. But you told me about Michael and how you'd decided you didn't want to be in a relationship, and I was afraid you'd reject me right away without giving me a chance or even listening to me. I thought that maybe if I gave you time to get to know me and if I tried to show you that I wouldn't leave you, it would make it easier for you to accept that not all guys are like Michael or your father."

Claude stopped in front of Andy. "You had no right to keep that secret to yourself," he said quietly. "Why did you agree to go along with this stupid fake relationship thing?" His eyes widened. "That night at the restaurant was a date, wasn't it?"

"Only if you want it to have been. I was just trying to get to know you, Claude. I knew you'd clam up if I told you that you were my mate because you expect me to want to be in a relationship with you."

"And you don't?"

Andy had no idea where to go from here. Claude wasn't as happy as he had been to realize they were mates, and he looked like he might say no, in spite of the bond that linked them together. None of Andy's brothers had been rejected by their mates, and it would destroy Andy to be the only one in that position.

He reminded himself that Jack had run, too. He'd left Blair behind, rejecting his mate temporarily, but Blair hadn't given up. He'd forged ahead, and now they were happy together.

Claude and Andy could have that, too. Andy had to believe

it.

He cleared his throat. "I didn't want to overwhelm you, especially with the party and the fact that you'd just learned about shifters. I wanted to give you time to wrap your mind around that, and I hoped you'd understand better what mates mean once you did."

"You told me what mates are," Claude pointed out.

"Then you know I'll never leave you."

"So what? We'll magically get along forever and be together for the rest of our lives?"

Andy had to resist the urge to laugh. Claude was angry, but he was giving Andy a chance to explain, which was all Andy had wanted. "No, that's not what it means. Even my parents fight and yell at each other sometimes. But they love each other and know that something bigger than both of them links them together. The bond between you and me means that we're two sides of a coin, two parts of the same soul. We can be apart, but we'll be happier if we're together. No matter how many times we fight, how many times you try pushing me away, I'm not going anywhere."

"You can't promise me that," Claude murmured.

But Andy could see he was softening up, or at least, he hoped that was what he was seeing. "I promise never to cheat on you. I promise that if there's ever a problem between us, I'll talk to you about it. I won't keep big secrets from you ever again. I'll work hard every day to make you happy and to keep our relationship as perfect as I can."

Claude was staring. Andy wasn't sure what else he could promise to get him to at least give him a chance. He was starting to feel desperate, and he didn't like the feeling that Claude was slipping between his fingers and out of his life.

He got to his feet. "I'm not like Michael. I wouldn't be even if you weren't my mate. I'm not a cheater, and if something isn't working in a relationship, I'd rather leave than hurt the person I'm with. I'm not asking you to marry me or anything like that. We've been getting along well, talking and texting, and I think it's a good sign of how our relationship could go. I just want you to give me a chance, Claude. I want you to give *yourself* a chance to be happy and to forget about Michael and what he did to you. I realize you're still hurt, and I don't blame you. You trusted him, and he broke that trust in the worst possible way. But again, I'm not Michael. I'm nothing like him, and I'll never do something like that to you."

Andy wasn't sure what else he could say. He needed Claude to believe him, but would he?

"But me being your mate doesn't mean we have to be together," Claude said.

Andy's heart broke. He was surprised he couldn't hear the sound of it cracking to pieces in his chest. "It doesn't," he confirmed.

"It doesn't mean you won't ever cheat on me or leave me."

"The only thing the bond does is show us that if we manage to make it work, we'll be the happiest we can ever be. It tells you that no one can make you as happy as I can if you give me a chance. I can't promise you we'll never fight, but I swear that if you give us a chance, I won't ever leave you. I'll work hard for our relationship and to make you happy. I realize you don't know me well, but you need to give yourself a chance to change that, and to give me a chance to show you that all of this is real. Just, please, say yes. Say yes to a date, more texting and calling, whatever you feel comfortable with. Say yes to *me*."

Claude stared at Andy for a moment. His expression was frozen, and while Andy had believed his heart had broken just a few seconds ago, he realized that wasn't true.

It was breaking now as Claude shook his head and opened his mouth to say, "I can't."

"Claude—"

"I'm sorry. I realize how important being with your mate is to a shifter, but I don't know if I can do this. It's not only Michael. It's also that none of my relationships have worked. None of my mother's relationships have, either. She's been hammering into my head that we're not built for relationships for years, and I started to believe her. I want what you're offering desperately, but I don't know if I can make myself take it. I'm terrified that if I do, I'll come to resent you and that I won't ever stop being afraid. I don't want to hurt you. You've been nothing but nice to me."

"Are you saying you never want to see me again?"

"I'm saying please, give me time to wrap my mind around all of this."

Claude hadn't said yes to Andy, but he also hadn't said no. It wasn't what Andy wanted, but it could have gone so much worse, and he was aware of that. He'd promised he'd give Claude time, and since that was what Claude was asking for, he nodded.

"I'll give you time. You have my number. Whenever you need to talk to me, use it. I won't try contacting you until you do, because you clearly need space. Just remember that I want this more than I've ever wanted anything in my life. I want *you* more than anything and anyone else." And hopefully, Andy would get him.

He didn't know what he'd do otherwise.

Claude was the first to leave. He hoped Andy would find his way back to the entrance of the building because he didn't feel up to taking him there. His heart was breaking, and it was entirely his fault, but he didn't know how to fix this.

Every single relationship Claude had in the past had ended badly. He'd been cheated on, stolen from, told he was more a friend than anything else. Every single time, a piece of his heart had hardened, or at least, that was what he'd believed. After Michael, he'd truly thought it was time for him to stay away from relationships and guys, and he'd thought he'd succeed. He hadn't thought any other guy would be able to make him feel the way he felt, but he hadn't counted on Andy.

And now, he'd abandoned Andy upstairs on the roof.

Part of Claude had been screaming at him to say yes to Andy. He wanted what Andy was offering, but he was also terrified of getting it. What if something changed between them? What if Andy eventually changed his mind? Yes, Claude was his mate, but Andy had confirmed that it didn't mean he'd be forced to stay with him. Besides, Claude wouldn't have wanted him to be. If Andy didn't want to be with him anymore, he should be able to leave.

But thinking about this was pointless because they weren't even together. Claude didn't have the guts to say yes and explore a relationship with Andy because of his past and because he was a coward. He'd felt the same way when he'd first met Michael. He'd been wary of relationships and had decided he was done, but then Michael had pushed his way into his life, and he'd decided to give love one last chance.

That chance had burned down, taking his heart with it. Could he really give someone else one last chance? Every time, he'd hoped it would be the last. He was disappointed and hurt every time, and he needed to learn to live on his own again.

And Andy was incredible. Claude was already falling for him, and he could only imagine how hard it would be when Andy decided to leave him. Why should he put himself through that once more? What would it change? He didn't want to hurt Andy or himself, but even being Andy's mate didn't guarantee happiness forever.

Claude reached his desk. He'd hoped Edgar had left, but he realized he was wrong when Edgar's office door flew open.

Edgar came through with a wide smile on his face. It quickly vanished when he saw that Claude was alone and probably looked like his dog had died.

"What happened?" Edgar asked as he strode closer. "Where's Andy?"

Claude shook his head. "You should have left by now."

"Why? What happened?"

"He told me I'm his mate."

Edgar sat on the edge of Claude's desk. Claude could feel his gaze on him, and he didn't want to look up. It was easier to stare at the floor.

"Is that a bad thing?" Edgar asked.

"I don't know. I don't know anything anymore. This was supposed to be easy, a fake relationship for the time of the party. When did it become more?"

"When you started falling for him."

Claude closed his eyes. He'd known Edgar could see it. "Did you know?" he asked in a whisper.

"That you were Andy's mate?"

"Yes."

"I did. He told me when he picked you up here to take you to dinner. I told him to be cautious, and I shared what your mother did to you."

Claude glared at him. "My mother didn't do anything to me."

"That's not true. She's not happy being single, but she can't find happiness with men, and she wants you to feel the same. She doesn't want to be alone in her misery, and it's not right."

"She doesn't make decisions for me. I'm the one who decided to tell Andy I couldn't be with him."

Edgar shook his head. "But why not? I understand you're afraid to get hurt, especially after what Michael did, but Andy isn't just another guy. You're his mate, and for a shifter, it means everything. I can't think of one mate couple who broke up. Mathilde and I are still together, as are Andy's parents. I'd bet both my kidneys that all of his brothers will still be with their mates thirty years from now. You could have that, Claude. If only you'd stop listening to your mother and her fears, you could have that."

That was all Edgar had to say, but Claude had already heard all that. Edgar had tried convincing him to give love a chance so many times that Claude had lost count. Every time, Claude listened to his mother instead.

But today, he was tempted to listen to Edgar.

Was he right? Did Claude's mother just want him to be as miserable as she was? She kept saying she didn't need a guy to be happy, but Claude didn't think she was.

He started packing his things, but on instinct, he grabbed his cell phone to call his mother. It took her a while to answer, and Claude didn't know what to tell her when she did.

"What is it?" she asked when he didn't say anything. "Claude? Are you all right?"

"I don't know," he said. "I met this guy, Andy. He's perfect. He really is, not like Michael. We went on a few dates, and everything was perfect, but I pushed him away when he told me he wanted more." Everything came out in a rush. Claude was careful not to mention shifters or mates because his mother didn't know anything about them, but she didn't need to. She could give Claude advice without knowing that Andy could turn into a black swan.

"I told you to stay away from men," she said. "You didn't listen, and now, you're hurt again."

"I'm hurt because I told him I couldn't be with him. He didn't cheat on me or dump me. I'm the one who did that."

"And you did the right thing. You'll realize it's for the best soon enough. You'll see."

Claude felt he'd never feel that way, though. He wasn't a shifter, but that didn't change the fact that he was Andy's mate. He'd never find another man like Andy, and he didn't want to look for one. He wanted Andy, no one else.

"Men are awful," his mother continued. "Well, except for you, of course. I know it hurts. It always does when you start falling in love. But it's better to take care of your heart and shield it from the pain that will come. Eventually, this guy of yours would have shown his true colors, and you'd have been in as much pain as you were when Michael cheated on you. I was right about him, wasn't I?"

"That's because you say that every guy I meet is going to dump me," Claude said, knowing he was being snarky but not caring one bit.

"And I'm right every time. I don't know this new guy, but I don't need to. If you give him a chance, he'll sneak into your life, take whatever he wants from you, then dump you once he has it. You don't need that kind of problem, Claude. You just need to focus on yourself and our family. Just look at me. I'm perfectly happy alone."

But Claude wasn't sure that was true, and even if it was, maybe it wasn't for him. Even if his mother could be happy alone, he wanted to love and be loved. He wanted to build a relationship and a life with someone, no matter how many times his heart could break.

He'd already gone through that pain. He knew what he stood to lose and what he could risk by giving Andy a chance. Would it really be that horrible to go through it one more time? Wouldn't it be worth it in case Andy was the right guy for him?

After all, Claude was Andy's mate. Every relationship Claude knew that involved mates was a happy one. Why was he so convinced that his relationship with Andy would be the only one that failed?

He still didn't have any answers when he hung up, but he could see what Edgar had been talking about when he mentioned Claude's mother's misery. She did want Claude to be as miserable as she was, but he was done with that.

If Andy gave him another chance, he'd take it.

But would Andy even want to talk to him?

CHAPTER SIX

It had been a week, and Andy still hadn't heard from Claude. He kept hoping his mate was calling every time his phone vibrated, but every time, he was disappointed, and he was so fucking done with this. He'd been miserable since he'd left Claude's office, and he didn't know how to get out of his funk.

Could he even get out of it? Claude wasn't just a guy who'd dumped him. He was Andy's mate, and Andy had never felt the kind of heartbreak he was going through with anyone else. He doubted he ever would again. This pain was all for Claude, all because Claude was his mate.

He sighed and stared at his phone on the coffee table. He desperately wanted to grab it, call Claude, and beg him to take him back. He'd promised Claude he wouldn't do that, but he didn't like feeling that he was giving up. He'd given Claude an entire week to think about this. Surely, the least Claude could do was to tell Andy what he'd decided, even if he never wanted to see him again? Andy wanted answers, and he wouldn't get them by staring at his phone.

He sat up straighter on his couch and grabbed his phone. He dialed Claude's number, which he already knew by heart, and waited for Claude to answer.

He didn't.

Before Andy could give himself time to think about what he was doing, he dialed the office number. He had to talk to three different people before he finally managed to get passed to Claude.

But it wasn't Claude who answered.

"Edgar Syme."

Andy had no idea what to say. He was supposed to talk to Claude, not to Claude's boss and Jack's father-in-law. "Hi. It's Andy, Jack's brother."

There was a moment of silence. "I see. You were looking for Claude?"

"Yes."

Edgar sighed. "He's not at his desk right now, but even if he were, I don't think I'd tell him about this phone call."

Andy winced. "I know. I realize I'm not doing the right thing. I was just desperate."

"I understand. I'm sorry he's treating you this way, but I don't think you should call him if he doesn't want to talk to you."

"I just wish he'd tell me he doesn't want me. He said that he needed time, and I've given him that. Why can't he tell me whether or not he can see a future with me?"

"I don't know. He's been moping around the office the entire week. I tried talking to him a few times, but he told me to stay out of his business. I can't say he's wrong. He's an adult, and he's not my son. I really do hope the two of you will be able to work things out, though. It's not right for mates to be separated."

Andy felt the same way, but he understood why Claude was so scared.

He was frightened, too. Even though Claude was his mate — or maybe because of it — it would be easy for him to break Andy's heart. He could stomp on it and reduce it to a million pieces like he had the day they'd talked on the roof, and Andy wouldn't be able to do anything to stop it. No matter what Claude felt, no matter what he'd said, Andy had already fallen for him, and nothing would change that. Even if he never saw Claude again, he'd always carry him in his heart. No one would ever measure up to Claude, and Andy didn't want anyone to try. If Claude didn't want him, he might give up on relationships like Claude had.

"I'll try talking to him again," Edgar said. "But distract yourself. I can't even imagine how much it hurts, but waiting by the phone won't help."

"What will?"

"I honestly have no idea. Hopefully, I'll be able to talk some sense into him."

Andy couldn't ask for anything else. "Thank you."

"Don't thank me yet. I'm not making any promises."

"But you're already doing much more than you're supposed to do. It's good to have you on my side."

"We all are. If I can't convince Claude to give you a chance, I'll have my wife deal with him."

That made Andy laugh. He hadn't laughed in a week, and he felt rusty.

But he had to remember that even if he never got his mate, he wasn't alone. He had his family, and eventually, he'd be able to fall in love again. It would take time, and it would never be what it could have been with Claude, but he'd deal with it when it happened.

For now, though, he wanted nothing more than to lick his wounds.

He and Edgar hung up, and Andy found himself staring at his phone again. Maybe Edgar was right, and he needed to do something different. An entire week staring at the phone hadn't changed Claude's mind, so maybe it was time for Andy to change his behavior.

He got up. He couldn't do anything about Claude, but he hadn't seen his brothers in way too long, and hopefully, they'd be enough to distract him. That usually worked, especially when it came to Jack, so Andy decided that was where he'd go.

It was early in the evening, but Jack had made a point of

going home early every day since Blair had moved in with him. That meant that when Andy parked his car in front of the house, he could see Jack was home, as well as Blair.

But they weren't alone.

Laurie's car was there, too, and Andy found himself smiling. He couldn't tell whether Melissa was with him, but he hoped so. Playing with his niece and taking care of her would surely help soothe the pain in Andy's chest.

He quickly knocked, then opened the door. "Is anyone home?" he called out as he took off his shoes and jacket.

Laurie peeked into the entrance from the living room. "Hey. Are you here for dinner?"

"I don't know. Are you?"

Laurie grinned. "I'm trying to convince Jack that he loves me enough to give me a plate of fried chicken, but I'm not sure I'm succeeding."

"That's because the fried chicken is all mine!" Jack called from the kitchen.

Laurie laughed. "Blair is cooking."

And it smelled delicious. Andy could do basic things like pasta and PBJs, but fried chicken? He'd sell his car if it meant he could get his hands on Blair's fried chicken.

"I'm staying for dinner, too," he called out.

"Good," Laurie said as they both walked into the living room. "I feel like I haven't seen you in ages."

Andy shrugged. "I've been busy, and so have you." He beamed at the sight of Melissa sitting on the floor. "Hey there, gorgeous. What are you doing?" He sat in front of her, crossing his legs. He was ready to start playing and forget all about Claude for as long as he could.

He could feel Laurie's gaze on him, but he ignored it and focused on the baby. She was growing so fast that he felt that she looked different every time he saw her. Or maybe it was him who was different this time around. He'd gotten his heart broken, and he didn't know how to fix it.

"Are you all right?" Laurie asked.

"I will be."

"Claude?"

Andy shook his head. "I don't want to talk about him."

"All right. But remember that if you need to talk, I'm here. We all are, and we'll all support you through whatever's happening between you and Claude."

Andy would need it, but he wasn't ready to talk about it and admit that Claude didn't want him. Soon, he'd have to tell his family.

But not now. Now, he'd play with Melissa and act as if everything in his life was perfectly fine. Then he'd go home, cry, and maybe, just maybe, finally start getting over Claude and the rejection that still hurt his heart.

Claude thought about Andy as he went back to his desk. He hadn't been able to focus on his work for an entire week, and he'd thought it would be a good idea to get a bottle of water and distract himself for a moment. The problem was that distracting himself from his job meant that he was thinking about Andy even more, so clearly, it *hadn't* been a good idea.

Claude wanted to talk to Andy, but he was terrified. He'd felt strong when he'd talked to his mother and had decided that no matter what she said, no matter what she thought, he could have Andy in his life. But by the time she was done talking to him, he'd shriveled into a tiny mess of a man who wasn't sure of anything anymore.

He wanted to give Andy a chance. He wanted the two of them to have the opportunity to be together, work things out, and hopefully be happy, but where should he start? He'd asked Andy for time to think about this, but no matter how much he did, his thoughts always circled back to one thing.

He was Andy's mate. It meant a lot to Andy, but would it be enough to keep Andy by Claude's side? Or would Andy eventually realize that he was better off without Claude and leave?

That was Claude's worst fear. If he gave in to Andy — and he desperately wanted to — what would happen if Andy left? Would there be anything left of his heart this time around?

So instead of calling Andy as soon as he'd hung up with his mother, Claude had waited. He was *still* waiting, and while he realized he was a coward, he had no idea how to change any of this. Could it be as easy as calling Andy and telling him he'd made his decision? The fact that they were living an hour apart didn't help, and Claude had used that, amongst other things, as an excuse.

When he got back to his desk, he found Edgar sitting in his spot. He frowned, mentally going over the work he should be doing. Was Edgar missing something that Claude had been supposed to take care of?

"Did you need anything?" he asked as he neared the desk.

Edgar squinted. "For you to stop being an idiot."

Claude took a step back, not having expected that. "I'm sorry?"

"Don't say you're sorry when you're not. What are you doing, Claude?" Edgar rose from his seat. He gestured at Claude to follow him into his office, and Claude had no choice but to do so. He didn't want half the office to hear whatever was happening, and they definitely would if he and Edgar stayed at his desk. He didn't have an office like Edgar. His desk was in an open space so that he could see people approaching, and he'd never disliked it, at least until now. It would be too easy for someone passing by to hear what Edgar was saying, and the entire office would know by the end of the meeting.

Claude stepped into the office, the tension high enough to make him want to run. He had to trust that Edgar wouldn't hurt him. He never had, and Claude didn't see a reason for him to start now. Still, this felt a bit too much like he might be about to get fired, which he didn't want to happen.

Edgar closed the door, then turned to Claude. "What are you doing with Andy?" he asked.

Claude blinked because that wasn't what he expected. "I'm sorry?"

"Stop being an idiot. You're his mate. You know how much it means to him. Why haven't you called him? Why have you told him you needed time?"

Claude crossed his arms over his chest and glared at his boss. "Why are you sticking your nose into this? Andy is part of my private life, and you have no say in it."

"I thought we were friends."

The quiet pain in Edgar's voice made Claude instantly feel guilty. "Of course we are," he said with a sigh. "And I'm sorry I snapped at you. The thing is that I have no idea what I'm doing, and I don't know how to answer your question."

Edgar nodded. "I get that. It's complicated, but then, relationships usually are. But, Claude, if you don't want Andy, you need to tell him. He's been waiting for you, and it's not fair to keep him waiting when you already know you won't be in his life."

"I never said I didn't want him," Claude whispered.

"But you've been behaving as if you don't. He's in pain and confused, and it's not right. He gave you time, and the least you can do is give him an answer."

Claude rubbed his face. "But I don't know what my answer will be."

"Then you need to make a decision. You can't keep him hanging for much longer."

He was right. Claude was being cruel to Andy, and Andy didn't deserve it. Claude didn't want him to be in pain, either. "Have you heard from him?" he asked. There had to be a reason Edgar was bringing this up now.

"He called your desk. He tried calling your cell phone first, but you left it there, and when he didn't get an answer, he tried the office. I picked up and explained that he needed to leave you alone, but I don't like any of this."

Claude swallowed. "I never meant to hurt him."

"I know, which is the only reason I haven't yelled at you. You're not the kind of person who would hurt someone like that willingly, but it doesn't mean this has been easy on him. Whatever your decision, you need to make it soon."

"Tell me about mates," Claude begged. "Do you really think that Andy will never leave me once we're together? Can it be as simple as that?"

Edgar stared at Claude for a moment before sitting in one of the armchairs in the sitting area in the corner of his office. He motioned to Claude to sit in the armchair next to his, and Claude did because why not? He was confused and worried, and he didn't know where to start. If Edgar helped him, maybe he'd be able to make his decision.

"The bond mates share doesn't guarantee a relationship," Edgar said slowly. "It just means that while you can be happy with other people, there's no one that can fit with you as well as your mate does. It's still work, though. You have to be there for your mate, to support them and love them. You have to share your life with them, make decisions together, and everything else. I know you're capable of all of that. I've seen you do it with Michael, and you put all of yourself in that relationship. Michael didn't deserve it and treated you badly, but that doesn't change the fact that you're a loving person and that you need more than you've been allowing yourself to have."

"Andy could hurt me so badly," Claude murmured.

"And I have no doubt he will. Eventually, you'll find things that you can't see eye to eye on. You'll fight, scream at each other, and make up. But that's the thing. Mates are important

to shifters. We only have one shot, and usually, we'll do everything we can to ensure that our mate is happy. We don't
want to jeopardize that relationship, because it would mean
losing our mate and the unique bond we share with them.
You'll hurt Andy as much as he'll hurt you. It doesn't mean
you can't work things out. As I said, it'll take work, *hard* work,
but I know you're more than capable of that. You just need to
believe in yourself, and even more, right now, you need to
believe in Andy."

Everything Edgar was saying sounded true, but it didn't
help. The fear was still there, and Claude wanted nothing
more than to give in to it, step away from all of this, and be by
himself.

But then he thought of Andy calling the office because he
wanted to know what was going on. Andy cared about him,
even though they weren't together, and Claude cared about
Andy.

It was already too late, wasn't it? Claude had tried keeping
Andy at arm's length so he wouldn't end up in the same mess
as he had with Michael, but he'd fallen in love anyway. Whatever happened or didn't happen between them, Claude
would still be hurt. Now he had to decide whether he'd keep
that pain close to his chest, or if he wanted to give love a
chance and see what happened. He knew what he wanted to
do, but he also knew what he was too afraid to do.

"Claude, please," Edgar said. "I love you like a son, and I
want you to be happy. I don't think you will be if you stay on
your own. You're not the kind of person who can be alone for
so long, and you're planning on being alone for the rest of
your life. That's not right. You need and deserve love, and so
does Andy."

Claude sucked in a breath. "What about my mother?"

Edgar made a disgusted sound. "I'll have words for her if
I ever see her again. But like I said before, I truly believe she

wants everyone to be as miserable as she is. That's not right, Claude. She can't put her life together long enough to have a full relationship, but it doesn't mean you should do the same. You both deserve love and a full life. Just because she can't let go of her pain for long enough to do so doesn't mean you shouldn't. So, what will you do?"

That was the question, wasn't it?

Being with his brothers helped Andy feel better. He couldn't shake the sadness and feeling that he'd lost everything, but he knew it would eventually pass.

He didn't think he'd hear from Claude at all. Claude was avoiding him, and Andy had already decided that he wouldn't call again. Claude had his number. He'd said he needed time, and when and if he came to a decision, he could easily reach Andy and let him know what was going on. Andy needed to stop hoping it would happen anytime soon.

Maybe Claude had decided that not talking to Andy would be enough for him to realize what was happening. He wasn't wrong. Andy could tell when he was being rejected, and this felt like a rejection. He just wished his mate had more regard for his feelings. He understood Claude was confused and hurt and didn't know what he wanted, but the same could be said for Andy, except for the last one. He knew what he wanted but also that he wouldn't get it.

A slap on his cheek made him jerk back. Melissa grinned at him, then tried to slap him again. He caught her tiny hand and squeezed gently, glaring at her with no heat. "You can't slap people," he said.

"She's been doing that often," Laurie said from the couch. "I've been trying to teach her not to, but she seems to take it as a reason to do it even more often. Sorry about that."

Andy shook his head. "It's fine. Maybe I did need some

sense slapped into me."

Laurie arched a brow. "Ready to talk about Claude?"

Andy wasn't sure he'd ever be ready to talk about his mate. He'd stayed mostly silent through dinner, and he'd been able to feel both Jack and Laurie staring at him with concern. They were worried, and he didn't blame them. He was worried about his heart, too, but he didn't see a decision or a way out of this. He couldn't contact Claude, and Claude was the only one who could decide what he wanted. For now, he seemed to have decided he didn't want anything to do with Andy, and Andy needed to accept that.

"Probably not," he admitted.

Laurie sighed and turned on the couch. He put his feet on the floor, leaning forward to hug Andy, who was leaning with his back against the couch as he sat on the floor. "I love you," he said.

"Love you, too." Andy knew he sounded a little choked up, but it didn't matter.

"I'm really sorry this is a mess. I only ever wanted you to be happy, and I truly think Claude could make that happen if he got his head out of his ass. The problem is that it's stuck so far up there, maybe too much for him to realize what's happening."

"You have a way with words," Andy teased.

"You know me."

Andy did. His brothers would all be there for him if he needed them, but Jack and Laurie were the ones Andy had always been closest to. They were the three youngest, so it made sense, and Andy was glad to have them.

"No matter what happens, you'll always have our family," Laurie murmured. He pressed his chin into Andy's shoulder. "I know it hurts to watch me and the others be happy in our relationships."

"I'd never ask any of you not to be."

"We all know that. But none of us would blame you if you decided to take a step back. As long as you remember that we're here for you and that we're family, we won't try to pull you back into our lives. Take some time. You need it, after what happened with Claude. Just remember that we'll always be here for you."

Andy nodded. He wasn't sure that stepping back from his family would help, though. As much as it hurt to watch his brothers being happy with their mates, he didn't begrudge them that, and he didn't want to lose them. Even if it was only temporary, it would add to the pain he already felt, and that didn't sound like a good idea.

The doorbell rang, which made Laurie lean back. He frowned, turning his attention to the door. "I wonder who it could be."

It was getting late, and both Laurie and Andy had started saying it would be better if they headed home. They were still here because they were comfortable, but Melissa was starting to droop, and she'd need her bed soon.

Andy heard Jack walk to the front door. It opened, but he couldn't catch what Jack and the person there were saying. No matter how hard he tried, he only heard soft voices, and he settled back against the couch.

Only to scramble to his feet when Jack came into the living room with Claude behind him.

"Claude?" Andy asked, almost bowling Melissa over in his haste.

She slapped his leg, and he couldn't berate her for it.

He leaned down to pick her up, hoping to use her as a buffer, but Laurie snatched her before he could.

"Melissa and I were just leaving," he said. He narrowed his eyes at Andy. "Let me know what happens. If you need any-thing, you know where to find me."

"Thanks. I'll text you." Andy wanted to beg his brother to

stay, but he understood why Laurie wasn't willing to do so. Besides, it wasn't like he'd be alone. They were in Blair and Jack's home, so they wouldn't be far.

Claude and Laurie nodded at each other, but Laurie was frosty. Andy almost told him not to be angry at Claude, but it wouldn't change his brother's mind or his feelings. Laurie was fierce, especially when it came to protecting their family.

"I'll leave the two of you alone," Jack said. "Just remember that we're right next door in the kitchen. Yell if you need anything."

Andy nodded, unable to answer with his voice. He shuffled his feet, wondering when things had become so awkward between him and Claude. They hadn't been that way before.

"I'm surprised Jack let me in," Claude murmured.

"He wouldn't take this away from me."

"He's a good brother."

"They all are. They only want what's best for me."

"And they're not sure that it's me."

Andy sighed. "Can you blame them? You didn't give them a reason to trust you. You've been ignoring me for an entire week, and I thought that you'd made your decision and had decided not to let me know. Ghosting me would be a sure way to make me see you don't want me."

Claude sighed. "I wasn't ghosting you."

"It sure felt like you were."

"Can I sit? I know we need to talk, which is why I'm here."

He wouldn't have driven all the way here just to dump Andy, right? Claude's presence was enough to spark hope in Andy's chest, but he was wary of trusting that hope. It was terrifying to think that maybe Claude had driven to Andy just to tell him they shouldn't be together.

Andy had no idea what to think anymore and no idea how to deal with any of this.

"Let's sit down," he said.

His mouth was dry as he settled on the couch, and it turned drier when Claude sat next to him. They weren't close enough to touch, but Andy would only have to reach out to get to his mate. He wanted to do exactly that, but instead he kept his hands in his lap and waited.

Claude huffed. "Maybe I should have texted you. It didn't feel right to talk about this on the phone or by text, but now, I realize it's hard for me to talk to you when you're next to me."

"Do you want me to shift?"

Claude frowned. "It would make things awkward."

Andy shrugged. "Whatever you need."

Claude stared at him for a moment. "Even though I treated you badly, you're still thinking about me before you think about yourself." He sounded in awe that Andy was doing that.

Andy leaned closer, still not touching his mate. "For you, I'd do pretty much anything. You're the first thing I think of in the morning and the last in the evening. Even though you have a hard time believing it, you're my life, Claude. I realize it's a lot, but I won't deny it, because it's the truth. However you feel, whatever you think, you're my mate, and to me, that means everything."

It was tempting to say yes to Andy's offer to shift, but Claude would have felt like a coward if he had. He needed to look Andy in the eyes as he did this, and that wasn't going to work if Andy was a swan. Besides, it would make things awkward. Andy would have to strip and shift. Then once he shifted back, he'd have to dress quickly. They might have had sex, but that didn't mean they were comfortable with each other that way yet.

Hopefully, they would be soon.

Claude hadn't wanted to do this on the phone, but he hadn't known where to find Andy. He had no clue where Andy lived, but since he knew how close Andy was to his brother Jack, he'd decided to head there. He hadn't wanted to risk calling Blair to ask about Andy and Blair not telling him. Besides, it would have given him too much time to think, which was his worst enemy.

He cleared his throat. "You should stay in your human form," he said.

Andy looked disappointed. He'd put out his heart, had told Claude that he was the most important thing in his life, and Claude had told him he could stay in his human form.

Claude was messing this up, and he was starting to panic. He needed it to go well, but to make that happen, he'd have to say the words that were stuck in his throat.

"I need to tell you about my mother," he said.

Andy blinked, clearly confused, but he didn't try to stop Claude.

Claude was grateful because he wasn't sure he'd have been able to start talking again if that had been the case. He looked away, still unsure how to deal with all of this.

"She was young when she had me. She got pregnant in high school, and both she and my father decided to keep me. I've never met him because he left her before I was born. He promised he wasn't going anywhere and that he'd be a father to me, but instead, he left. He lied, and it hurt her. She had to raise me on her own. It was her and me for the longest time."

Claude cleared his throat. He understood why his mother was bitter. "When I left for college, she was lonely. She'd been single for twenty years, and I guess she was ready to give it a try again. She was in her late thirties when she met another guy. I was happy for her. They moved in together, and then one day, she told me she was pregnant. She really thought she'd have the family she'd always dreamed of. Instead, her new boyfriend left, just like my father had. He told her he didn't want a child, but she decided to keep my sister anyway, so he got out. This second betrayal was too much for her. She decided that men were all the same and that she was better off without one. She knew I was gay, and every time I had a boyfriend, she started telling me that he'd never love me, that I needed to dump him, and that I had to be careful with my heart, that any guy I'd be with would destroy it. Unfortunately, that proved to be true."

Claude was startled when Andy reached for his hand. Andy hesitated, but when Claude didn't move away, he linked their fingers together and squeezed. That was all he did, but it was still enough to make Claude feel supported.

"I've always wanted love. In the beginning, I didn't believe what she told me. I was convinced that eventually I'd find my prince charming. But with every relationship that ended badly, I wondered if she was right. I didn't want to believe I was destined to be on my own, but she kept telling me that the people in our family are disasters when it comes to relationships and that it was better to steer away from them entirely. I was hurt every time I lost someone, but I tried again and again. When I met Michael, I'd already decided he'd be my last attempt at being happy with a man. I thought I wouldn't need another."

"And he cheated on you and hurt you."

There was a growl in Andy's voice. He sounded like he wanted to find Michael and beat him up, and while Claude would never condone something like that, it made him happy.

"He did. After that, I told myself that my mother had to be right, and that was that. I gave up on relationships and thought I was doing the right thing." Claude still wondered if it would be better for him to stay away from Andy, but he'd decided to stop letting fear of getting hurt guide his steps.

Edgar was right. Claude's mother had allowed her pain to influence her, and as a result, she was still alone, even though Claude suspected she didn't want to be. He wasn't going to be like her, unwilling to give it a try. She had an entire life to find someone else to make her happy. The only reason she hadn't yet was that she was too bitter to let anyone in.

Claude didn't want to be bitter and angry. He wanted to be happy, and Andy would make that happen.

"I'm sorry she had to go through all that," Andy said slowly. "And I'm sorry it influenced the way you view relationships."

"It wasn't all her. The way my relationships went contributed."

"I know Michael hurt you badly. I can't promise you I won't ever hurt you, but I'll never cheat on you, Claude. I'll never treat you badly or disrespect you."

"I know."

"Good. I'm not sure what's going on, though. I'm glad you told me about your mother, but honestly, at this point, I'm afraid to ask what it means."

Claude forced himself to look at Andy. Andy deserved nothing less. "It means that even though I'm terrified, I decided to give this one last try. It's too late for me not to be hurt by your absence in my life. I realized I'd fallen in love with you already, although I don't know when it happened. But even if I tell you I never want to see you again, it will hurt because I love you."

There. The words were out, and it was Andy's turn to say something. Claude didn't think he'd ever been so afraid. He'd told himself he'd never make himself vulnerable again, yet here he was. Hopefully, it would be the last time. Claude might become a monk or a hermit if things didn't work out. He doubted he'd ever want to see a man again if Andy told him no.

Instead of telling Claude what he wanted, Andy pulled him closer. He dropped Claude's hand and wrapped both of his arms around Claude, holding him close. Claude let go, and a few tears rolled down his cheeks. He wanted Andy to hug him, but he wanted Andy to tell him what was going on even more.

He tilted his head up to do just that, but he didn't have a chance to say anything. Andy kissed him, and Claude couldn't *not* kiss him back.

He'd thought he'd lost any chance at this happening, and his heart felt like it was about to burst with happiness and the knowledge that he hadn't. He still needed words, though, and when he and Andy separated, he leaned back.

"What does this mean?" he asked.

"That this is it, for both of us. I'm never letting you go now that I have you, Claude. You're my mate, and no matter what your mother believes, I'll never leave you. I'll never cheat on you or betray you. I love you."

The tears came down harder, but Claude didn't care. He was in Andy's arms, safe, and that was never going to change for as long as he was alive.

CHAPTER SEVEN

Claude stared at the front door. Andy knew he was nervous, but no matter how many times he told Claude he shouldn't be, Claude had been a mess since they'd left his apartment.

"What if they don't like me?" Claude asked.

Andy had to suppress a smile. He didn't want to look like he was amused, even though in a way, he was. It touched him that Claude wanted his family to like him, but he really didn't need to be so worried about it.

"They've already met you, and they liked you," he pointed out.

Claude shook his head. "They didn't meet me as your mate. Besides, considering the mess I made of this entire situation, I wouldn't be surprised if they didn't want to see me again. I'm pretty sure Jack tried to kill me the other day."

This time, Andy did laugh. "He didn't try to kill you."

"He flew right at my face."

Andy wrapped an arm around Claude's shoulders and pulled him close so he could kiss his temple. "He didn't do it on purpose." Although Andy wasn't entirely sure about that. He and his brothers were expert flyers, and it hadn't made sense for Jack to fly right at Claude's face. Still, he'd promised he would never do it again, and Andy believed him.

Things between him and Claude had been going somewhat smoothly. It wasn't easy to deal with the distance, but Claude had been spending as much time with Andy as he could. That meant he'd stepped back from his job a bit, but

116

from what he'd told Andy, Edgar didn't care. If anything, he kept throwing Claude out of the office and telling him to take a day off, which always delighted Andy. He wanted more time with Claude, and eventually, that would come. But they were still in the beginning of their relationship, and neither of them was ready to leave their home behind.

Andy couldn't lie, at least to himself. He hoped Claude would eventually decide to move to their small town, mostly because he didn't want to leave his family behind. It was a decision they'd have to make together, and things between them were still a bit unsteady. Andy wouldn't be surprised if they ended up fighting over it, but the thought of fighting with Claude was enough for him to decide to table the conversation for now. First, they had to deal with this family dinner Claude was nervous about.

"They loved you when they met you, and that's not going to change," Andy told Claude. "Besides, even though you were a bit of an asshole, they're aware we talked and that we're together now. I'm not saying Jack won't continue to give you the cold shoulder for a few weeks, but once he sees how happy I am, he'll stop."

Claude squinted. "You really are happy?"

"Happier than I ever thought I could be." And that was the truth. Andy hadn't been looking for a relationship, and he hadn't needed one, but he was glad he had Claude. He'd promised himself that he'd never do anything that could put their relationship in danger, and that was how he'd been behaving since their chat. It had only been a few weeks, but he couldn't imagine his life without Claude anymore.

Before they could go in, Claude's phone rang. Edgar and his wife weren't attending this dinner, but they knew about it, so Andy hoped Edgar wasn't calling for work. He'd been hinting at Claude moving and becoming Blair's personal assistant, but that was another thing Claude and Andy hadn't talked about it.

Claude took out his phone and groaned. "It's my mother."

Andy held his breath. Claude had been avoiding his mother since they'd gotten together, but he wouldn't be able to do so forever. Andy couldn't help but be worried Claude wouldn't be strong enough to tell his mom he was in a steady relationship. He'd already warned Andy that she wouldn't be happy and that she'd try to get Claude to dump him, but Andy had faith in his mate. Now that he'd made his decision, he was a steady presence in Andy's life, and nothing his mother could say would change that.

Or at least, Andy hoped so.

"I could ignore the call," Claude said.

"Or you could tell her that you'll talk to her later because you're having dinner with your boyfriend's family."

Claude stared at the screen for a moment longer. "You know what? Fuck it. That's exactly what I'm going to tell her."

He answered so quickly that Andy didn't have the time to tell him he'd been joking.

Maybe he hadn't been, at least not entirely. Andy did want Claude to tell his mother about him. He just didn't want to push Claude into doing so before he was ready.

"Hey," Claude said. He lowered the phone and put it on speaker so Andy could hear the other side of the conversation.

"Finally," a woman said. "I was getting worried. Why haven't you been answering your phone?"

"I've been busy."

"Edgar is running you ragged?" She didn't sound happy about that.

"No. It has more to do with my new boyfriend."

There was a moment of silence. Andy wondered what Claude's mother was about to say, but he didn't have to wait for long.

"Oh, Claude. Don't tell me you fell for it again."

"I did, and you know what? I've never been happier."

"It won't last for long. It never does."

"It will this time." Claude straightened his back, ready to face his mother. "And I need you to stop talking like that. I'm not you. I've been hurt by men before, but that pain wasn't enough to get me to stop looking for love. I've found it, and I'm happy. I need you to be happy for me, not to tell me I'll get dumped in a few weeks."

Andy grabbed Claude's free hand and squeezed. He wanted Claude to know that he'd never do that. Whatever happened in their future, they'd face it together.

"But that's how you always feel in the beginning," Claude's mother protested.

"Maybe, but it doesn't mean things are going to break down. I know this relationship will work, and I need you to accept that. You might be better off on your own and happier, but that's not the case for me. I want love, and I have it now. I don't want to end up like you, bitter and alone. Andy and I are together, and that's that."

"I just want to keep you safe."

"But you're not doing so by telling me I'll never be loved. I'm sorry, but I need to go. I'm having dinner with him and his family. Think about what I said, okay? I won't call you, and I hope that you'll at least accept this by the time you decide to call me."

Claude hung up without giving his mother the time to add anything. He sucked in a breath, then another, and pushed his phone into his pocket. Then he turned and smiled at Andy. The smile was tense and awkward, but he was trying. "Sorry about that," he said.

Andy pulled him closer and kissed him gently. "Don't apologize. I already knew she wouldn't take this well."

"It's frustrating, you know? I want her to be happy for me, but instead, she keeps telling me this won't last."

"It will."

"I know." Claude seemed to believe it now.

Andy was glad. He realized it would take time, because no matter how many times he told Claude he loved him and that he wasn't going anywhere, he wasn't the first one to do so. The only way to fully convince Claude that he was telling the truth was to do what he was saying. He'd stand by Claude's side for the rest of Claude's life, and eventually Claude would know that Andy would never leave him.

"I love you," Andy said.

Claude's smile was more natural now. "I love you, too. Shall we go in? After talking to my mother, I feel ready to face anything."

Andy kissed Claude again, then allowed his mate to pull him toward the house.

Things weren't perfect, but he didn't need them to be. He loved Claude, and Claude loved him, and they both had to trust their heart. They were young and had all the time in the world to figure things out.

And they would — together.

ABOUT THE AUTHOR

Catherine is the creator of several series, most of them paranormal, including the Whitedell Pride Series and the Gillham Pack Series. While she graduated in translation, she decided to go the writer's way because it was more fun to create her own stories and characters.

She's been living in Italy for more than twenty years, but she's a daughter of the North—Belgium to be precise—and she misses it so much that she's already planning to move back.

She loves pizza—probably too much—her son, her pets, and of course, books. She sneaks some reading time into her schedule every time she has five minutes free from writing, demands from her various pets and son, and lastly, housework.

Connect with her:

lievens.catherine@gmail.com
BookBub: https://www.bookbub.com/authors/catherine-lievens
Website: https://authorcatherinelievens.com/
Facebook: https://www.facebook.com/catherine.lievens.9
Facebook Group: https://www.facebook.com/groups/411788002341528/
Twitter: https://twitter.com/authorCLievens
Newsletter: http://eepurl.com/c-uvKn

www.ingramcontent.com/pod-product-compliance
Lightning Source LLC
Chambersburg PA
CBHW071626140626
46555CB00021B/854